Closer and closer he came, riding his black, spirited mustang with an easy grace. The closer he got, the more fantastic he seemed. Who was he?

When the horse reared, the man stayed in control, his powerful thighs gripping the horse's flanks. He looked like the quintessential cowboy, a Marlboro man without the cigarettes.

"That cowboy can hang his lariat on my bedpost any night of the week," Sandra's friend said.

He dismounted in a swoop, then came to Sandra, a firm smile curving his lips. His turquoise eyes linked with hers and Sandra felt as though she were the only woman in the world.

"Sandra," he whispered in a low, musical voice. "I thought you'd never get here."

ABOUT THE AUTHOR

Cassie Miles lives in Denver with her two teenage daughters. She's written many Harlequin novels and has long been a steady contributor to the Intrigue series. While she continues to write romantic mysteries for Harlequin, she is pleased to offer her first American Romance novel— and a hero, Buffalo McCloud, whom she hopes you'll love!

Books by Cassie Miles

HARLEQUIN INTRIGUE

HARLEQUIN TEMPTATION

Cassie Miles

BUFFALO McCLOUD

Harlequin Books

TORONTO • NEW YORK • LONDON
AMSTERDAM • PARIS • SYDNEY • HAMBURG
STOCKHOLM • ATHENS • TOKYO • MILAN
MADRID • WARSAW • BUDAPEST • AUCKLAND

ISBN 0-373-16567-6

BUFFALO McCLOUD

Chapter One

Following her regular after-work swim at the posh downtown Denver Athletic Club, Sandra Carberry toweled dry and wrapped herself in a short terry-cloth robe. In the gleaming, tiled locker room, she blow-dried her blond hair that fell neatly to her shoulders. The public address system in the locker room paged her in a low, tasteful voice.

She picked up a courtesy phone. "This is Sandra Carberry."

"There's a gentleman at the front desk who would like to see you. His name is Russel McCloud."

"McCloud?" She didn't recall anyone by that name. "What does he look like?"

There was a wait before the woman who worked at the reception area said, "He's standing right across the lobby, and I guess I could say... Well, he's, he's kind of incredible."

"Could you be a bit more specific?"

Her voice lowered to a breathy whisper. "Tall. Black hair, blue eyes. Shoulders..."

"Yes?" Sandra laughed. "He has shoulders?"

"Shoulders to die for. He has a black cowboy hat with a silver band. And his Levi's. Well, they fit like a chamois glove."

"I get the general idea." Though Russel McCloud wasn't a name Sandra recalled, the description sounded fairly unforgettable. "Please ask him to wait. I'll be out in a minute."

Sandra hurried to the walnut-paneled dressing area where she quickly applied her simple makeup and dabbed on a hint of perfume. The scent seemed too heavy and musky after her healthy swim, but she was confident that the fragrance was pure sophistication because she'd paid a small fortune for a dinky little vial of it.

Almost ready, she slipped into her brand-new, elegantly draped, white silk dress. The moment she'd spotted this designer frock at Saks, she'd known it was exactly right for the occasion. Tonight was special. Tonight, in the penthouse lounge of Denver's thirty-story Apollo Building, she would be formally welcomed as a partner in the prestigious law firm of Jessop, Feldner and White.

Sandra allowed herself a self-satisfied grin. In the six short years since she'd graduated from law school, she'd gone from struggling beginner to Professional with a capital *P,* which she hoped would soon be joined by other significant letters: BMW on her car, YSL on her luggage and VIP whenever anyone mentioned her name.

After storing her other clothes in her locker and grabbing her fawn leather briefcase, she whisked onto the main floor of the club where the ambiance suggested high tea at a respectable English manor house. The woman at the front desk sat up a little straighter when she spotted Sandra. "I'm sorry, Ms. Carberry, if my comments seemed out of line."

"No problem. Where is this incredible Mr. McCloud?"

"He said he'd wait for you out front. By the way, the *Cinco de Mayo* celebrations have already started, and downtown is a mess."

"Thanks for the warning."

When Sandra opened the heavy oak door, she heard the twanging echo of a mariachi band. *Cinco de Mayo,* the Fifth of May, was Mexican Independence Day and a big event in Colorado, celebrated with fireworks and dancing, piñatas and parades. Though she usually enjoyed the spectacle, the festivities seemed like an inconvenience tonight, an obstacle to reaching her building on the other side of the Sixteenth Street Mall.

She hoped the man who stood at the bottom step of the entry to her club would not be another hindrance. Even if he were as amazingly virile as the receptionist seemed to think, Sandra was an attorney and half the people she met were adversaries.

"Mr. McCloud?"

He doffed his black cowboy hat, turned his head and looked up at her. His face was darkly tanned, weathered to perfection against high cheekbones. His hair was thick, black and shining. And his eyes... She inhaled a shallow gasp as she met his gaze. His eyes were turquoise blue.

"Hello, Sandra."

The unusual shade of blue was breathtaking, and the expression in those eyes startled her. Warm and wise and strangely intimate. As if he saw no one but her. As if she'd become the center of a very special universe.

Sandra cleared her throat. "Have we met?"

"No, but I feel like I know you."

She felt the same way.

"I wanted to meet you in person," he explained. "And this was convenient because I always come to Denver for *Cinco de Mayo.*"

"Cinco de Mayo?" She had completely forgotten the hundreds of people shouting and dancing in the street. Her awareness of her surroundings had melted, leaving only Russel McCloud's presence behind. If Sandra had believed in destiny, she would have thought this man had been sent specifically to fulfill her private longing for a partner, a significant other who would make her life complete. When she looked into his remarkable eyes, she realized how very much she needed someone in her life. She needed a man who would share her triumph at the law firm, who would share her happiness, who would share her bed. It was all too easy to imagine McCloud as that man.

Sandra blinked, but she couldn't erase the sensual images he provoked with no effort. He was all male. Broad across the chest, lean in the hips. The receptionist at the Athletic Club had been right about those shoulders.

"I know your parents," he said.

Sandra's fantasies crashed back to earth. Her parents, Emma and Thornton Carberry, were charming creative people. An artist and a poet. Though Sandra loved them dearly, they had nothing, absolutely nothing, in common with her own career-oriented life-style. Any friend of theirs had to be irresponsible, erratic and eccentric. Even if he did have amazing turquoise eyes.

Reluctantly, she took a step backward, away from McCloud. "It's been a long time since my parents tried to fix me up with a blind date. The last one was a drummer with a Hari Krishna band. All that chanting..."

"I'm not a blind date," he said.

"No?"

"We're both too mature for that."

"Right." Still, she was hesitant. Maturity was not a trait that her parents cultivated among their acquaintances. "So what's the catch?"

His eyebrows raised. "I don't know what you mean."

"Why are you here?" She was terribly disappointed that he hadn't materialized to fulfill her dreams. If he was sent by her parents, he had to be trouble. Brusquely she surmised, "Are you looking for free legal advice? Do you need a place to stay tonight? Did good old Emma and Thornton suggest that you might sleep on my sofa?"

"I'm not looking for a handout. Or a sofa." His voice was deep and commanding. The tone would have been too stern if he hadn't softened his words with a smile. "If I decide to sleep at your place, Sandra, it'll be on my terms."

That sounded like a promise. Or a threat. Her confusion mounted, leaving her uncharacteristically tongue-tied. "Then why..."

"Your parents asked me to deliver these papers to you." He picked up a large brown envelope that had been resting on the steps of the Athletic Club.

She accepted the battered package that was marked with her mother's artistic flourish and a small sketch of a roadrunner. The paper smelled faintly of turpentine and oils. As she slipped the package inside her briefcase, Sandra muttered, "I suppose Emma has some reason for not using the U.S. mail."

"I volunteered for the job," he said. "I wanted to meet the little girl who memorized the beginnings of the *Iliad* and *A Tale of Two Cities* before she was five years old."

"My father told you that." An embarrassed warmth crept up her throat. Why did parents always dwell on cutesy childhood exploits?

"He told me you were special, very bright. By the time you were seven, you knew all the capitals of Europe."

She scowled, not wanting to be thought of as a child by this very sexy man. "I was obnoxiously precocious. It's fortunate that I've managed to grow up."

"Yes, you have. Your dress," he said, while his gaze lingered, "is very formal."

"I thought the white was appropriate. The color worn by graduates and brides." Why was she talking about brides? Though her embarrassment had not abated, she'd gone from speechless to babbling. "Or maybe by a sacrificial virgin. You know, like in *King Kong*. The sacrificial females were clad in white before King Kong carried them off into the jungle."

"And is that what you're expecting this evening?"

"No, of course not."

"I'm glad." He grinned. "It'd be a shame to see you carried off by a giant ape."

"Or whatever it is that people do with virgins these days."

She couldn't believe she'd just blurted out something about virgins and King Kong. *Get a grip, Sandra.* She glanced down at her slim gold wristwatch. Thirteen minutes until seven. The cocktail party would be starting soon. "I have to rush. I have a previous engagement."

"I know. A cocktail party in your honor."

She shot him a surprised glance. Clearly, McCloud knew more about her than she knew about him, and that gave him an edge. "Did my parents tell you?"

"Yes, and I also talked to your secretary, Michelle, before she left the office. She was the one who told me I could find you at the Athletic Club. It seems, Sandra, that you are a creature of regular habit."

"I keep to a schedule," she said.

"Very practical."

She detected a note of disapproval in his voice, as if being practical, on time and focused were negative traits. But, of course, she would expect that attitude from one of her parents' friends. Her heels clicked down firmly on the pavement and she set her face toward the east, away from the setting sun. "Nice to meet you, Mr. McCloud."

"I'll walk with you."

They approached the colorful mass of people on the Sixteenth Street Mall. There were mariachis and individual guitarists howling "Malagueña." Many of the women wore brightly embroidered skirts. Though there were serapes and sombreros, most of the men were dressed like McCloud—in jeans, cotton shirts and cowboy hats.

Sandra was a bit annoyed that here, in her own city, she felt out of place in her sophisticated white dress. "So, McCloud, if you are a friend of my parents, you must be a starving artist. Or struggling with the great American novel."

"I'm a rancher. I raise buffalo."

"Unusual."

"But profitable," he said.

Her hopes elevated. Was it possible that her parents had actually met a man who had some sense of cash flow, some idea of reality? "And where is your ranch located?"

"Not far from Alamosa. At the foot of the San Juans."

Sixteenth Street Mall was clogged with dancers. Sandra tried to press forward, but this spirited folk dance covered the entire street and spilled across the blockaded intersection.

McCloud leaned close so she could hear what he was saying. "Easier to dance than to shove."

"Dance?" Her high-heeled pumps of fine Italian leather were not made for stomping and kicking. The line of her dress was narrow. She certainly didn't want to show up at the cocktail party all ruffled and sweaty. Dance? That wasn't a great idea.

But then she glanced up into his face. She'd never seen lips so inviting. A gaze so compelling. Her arm lifted and she rested her hand on his broad muscular shoulder. "Why not?"

He firmly clasped her waist and dragged her into the party. They twirled in a formless dance that vaguely resembled an upbeat polka. The crowd around them blurred into a kaleidoscope of bright color and light-hearted music, and in the center was McCloud. His turquoise eyes sparkled, enticing her toward spontaneous excitement.

Sandra threw back her head and laughed. As if she didn't have a care in the world. As if she wasn't about to be made partner at Jessop, Feldner and White.

The light touch of his callused hands sent a shiver from her fingertips to her brain. He lifted her in a twirl and her feet, lighter than air, left the ground. Her cheeks warmed, not from exertion as much as from an excitement she felt building inside her. When he pulled her close to his chest for a final swirl on the opposite side of the Mall, her heart thrummed in time with the music.

It wasn't until they reached the relative quiet of Seventeenth Street, Denver's financial district, that she caught her breath. She was surprised to see the seriousness of his expression when she felt so magnificently carefree.

Impulsively, she said, "Come with me, McCloud. To the cocktail party." She eyed his casual attire. He wasn't properly dressed, but it didn't matter. Even in Levi's, he was dazzling. "You don't have to change."

He hesitated, and she read a sadness in his gaze. "You're married," she concluded. "Or engaged. Or involved."

"No."

"Then why not? I'd love to share tonight with you."

"To share the night?" His voice caressed her. "I'd like that. Very much."

An impulse jolted through her. *Run away with him. Spend the night with him. Forget about Jessop, Feldner and White.* She could drown her responsibilities in his penetrating eyes.

"Sandra, have you ever heard of El Dorado? The Seven Cities of Gold?"

What a strange thing to ask! "Gold? I don't—"

"I'll explain to you. Another time."

She wanted to know when that time would come. As an attorney, she wasn't coy about making appointments and arranging her agenda. But she didn't feel professional around McCloud. He made her feel like a woman.

He clasped her right hand and gave a slight but firm tug, drawing her toward him. His eyes mesmerized her, pulling her irresistibly closer and closer until they were only a few scant inches apart. Her breasts grazed his chest, sending a fierce heat throughout her nervous system. Before she had time to consider, his lips met hers. Briefly, gently, like the kiss of a butterfly wing.

Then he moved away. "*Adiós*, Sandra."

He was gone.

She touched her lips. Had she really kissed a stranger, allowed him to kiss her? Or had her imagination run wild? Standing alone on the sidewalk in the dusky shadow of the Apollo Building, she felt bereft, alone and disheveled. She'd been swept off her feet.

Nonetheless, Sandra decided, she'd been lucky enough to land in one piece. And now, she needed to pull herself back together. She pushed through the revolving door.

Instead of riding the elevator all the way to the penthouse lounge, she disembarked on the eighteenth floor where her office was located behind the carved door with the gold-plated lettering for Jessop, Feldner and White.

Sandra hurried blindly through the deserted office maze and went through the door with her own nameplate upon it. Inside her office, she opened the narrow closet where a mirror was fixed at eye level on the door. She stared into it. Her lipstick was smeared. This was evidence she had been kissed.

Her fingers fumbled as she opened her briefcase and took out her small clutch purse. When she found her lipstick, she was trembling too much to touch the color to her lips. The Fates had been cruel. Finally she'd met the perfect man. A real man. And he'd vanished.

Exerting her willpower, she tried to erase McCloud's image from her mind. Tonight was important. Becoming a partner was the crowning achievement of her career, and she would not allow her celebration to be ruined by a stranger she would probably never see again.

Sandra removed from her briefcase the battered envelope from her parents. She opened the top flap and removed a sheaf of papers. The first page was a sheet of heavy parchment, a letter from her father.

After salutations, he'd written, *By the time you read this, your mother and I will be in Africa on a cultural exchange program. We'll be gone for three months, and I enclosed an itinerary which may or may not be useful because you know how often our journeys take us off the beaten path.*

Sandra frowned as she read. Why hadn't they telephoned to let her know about this trip?

We tried to reach you before our departure, the letter continued, but the only voice I heard was on your answering machine.

One of her father's quirks was that he refused to leave messages on machines.

His letter went on to say that Emma and Thornton had made many changes in recent weeks, and they would appreciate if she went over the paperwork. In conclusion, Thornton Carberry congratulated her on becoming a partner. *But remember, Sandra, legalities are not always justice. And truth comes from within your heart.*

"Thanks, Dad," Sandra said quietly. At least his sentiment had merit, and she agreed with him. Ethics were important in every profession, especially law. She glanced back at the letter. What were these changes he referred to? Later. She would have to find out later.

She smoothed her blond hair and straightened the line of her white silk dress. With her features arranged in an expression of cordial confidence, she ascended to the penthouse lounge where the other partners and lawyers and senior secretaries raised their fluted champagne glasses in salute. Though her ears rang with their congratulations, McCloud's voice whispered seductively in the back of her mind, *Have you ever heard of El Dorado?*

OVER THE WEEKEND, while she reviewed the papers in the battered envelope, Sandra learned more than she'd ever wanted to know about the mythical cities of gold.

It seemed that Emma and Thornton Carberry had sold their successful boardinghouse and retreat on twenty-five acres near Cripple Creek, Colorado. With the profits—which were considerable because the area had recently legalized gambling and property values had gone sky-high—her parents had invested in an archaeologist who was mounting a search for these cities of gold.

"An archaeologist," she muttered as she dropped the contracts on her coffee table. "And a buffalo rancher."

McCloud!

Though the cold, hard facts indicated that McCloud was nothing more than a con man who had sweet-talked her parents out of a significant portion of their life savings, Sandra couldn't erase her remembrance of his turquoise blue eyes. Nor had her lips forgotten the subtle finesse of his kiss.

She wasn't the sort of woman who enjoyed casual hugging and friendly pecks on the cheek. Physical contact should mean something. In her eyes, a kiss was not "just a kiss."

And she didn't believe that McCloud had intended for their fleeting embrace to be a mere goodbye to a new acquaintance. Or to soften her up for the contracts she'd find in her briefcase. He'd been compelled, just as she had. Whether or not she liked it, an element of fate had come into play.

But that kiss would have to be destiny deferred. Russel McCloud had connived her parents into investing six hundred thousand dollars on a search for El Dorado. Three hundred thousand in their own names, and one hundred thousand each for their three children.

Sheer lunacy! She certainly hoped he would be reasonable when she discussed the matter with him. If he wasn't willing to issue a refund, she would insist that the money be placed in an escrow account pending the return of her parents from Kenya.

It should be simple. Sandra would apologize with a simple "sorry for the misunderstanding, but my parents are lunatics." And a "good luck with your search." And it would be concluded neatly.

First thing on Monday morning, she telephoned his ranch. His voice over the phone echoed with a deep timbre that gave her shivers, but Sandra wrapped herself in cool, reserved professionalism. "It seems," she said, "that my parents have invested a great deal of money with you."

"I've been thinking of you, Sandra."

She gulped hard, swallowing an impulse to go all goopy inside. No matter how charming and sexy he might be, they were talking about a potential loss of six hundred thousand dollars, which was certainly enough cold hard cash to put the freeze on any sort of lamebrain attraction she might be feeling toward him. "According to these contracts, the amount my parents allocated to your alleged quest was—"

"Did you enjoy the rest of *Cinco de Mayo?*"

"Certainly." Sandra hadn't left her condo for the rest of the weekend. She'd been locked indoors, reviewing the documents her parents had left with her and preparing queries for a Tuesday deposition on a difficult case. "Listen, McCloud, my parents signed these documents without benefit of legal counsel. Some of the terms are unclear and I believe the best course for all of us is to abort the contact. Immediately."

When he laughed, her overactive imagination conjured visions of a wild free wind chasing clouds across a blue sky. She blinked frantically. She'd be damned if she allowed this southern Colorado buffalo rancher to brush her off with a chuckle and a pat on the head. "This isn't a joke, McCloud."

"What's the capital of Liechtenstein?"

"Vaduz," she replied automatically. "Stop it!"

"Belgium?"

"I'm not playing. And I don't appreciate being thought of as a little girl who once memorized a bunch of European capital cities."

"I don't think of you as a girl, Sandra. You're very much a woman."

"And a professional."

He sighed heavily. "If you insist."

"McCloud, we need to come to an understanding about my parents' so-called investment."

"Do you remember what I told you when we met?"

"Specifically?" She recalled a great deal about his kiss, but his words were vague. "No."

"If we decide to spend more time together, it will be on my terms."

The phone went dead.

She redialed, but her call was picked up by an answering machine.

Chapter Two

The man was arrogant, infuriating and…unavailable.

Over the next several days, Sandra left dozens more messages on his machine and with various members of his staff at the ranch, but McCloud never called back. Not once! Not even a courtesy call telling her to jump off the proverbial bridge. What a pig! She wouldn't let him get away with this behavior.

On Friday morning, she took off from work and flew on a puddle jumper to Alamosa, the nearest town to McCloud's ranch. Though he wasn't at the ranch when she arrived unannounced, Sandra was far too angry to wait. That wasn't her style. Why leave well enough alone when she could wade into the center of battle? That was why she'd become a lawyer in the first place. Injustice outraged her. And she was thoroughly convinced that her parents had been conned.

She meant to set things right. And she meant to do it today. Though the stablehand scoffed at her chances of finding McCloud in these miles of high plains at the foot of the San Juans, she convinced him with sheer determination and fifty dollars in cash. He loaned her a horse named Pansy.

Though Sandra had ridden horseback before, it had been years ago. Twelve years ago, at least. She'd ridden frequently during the summer when her parents had taken the family to live in an artists' commune near Santa Fe, which was not all that far from here as the crow flies.

After five hours—which seemed like fifty years—of jostling on Pansy's rump, Sandra stopped atop a mesa and scanned a wide valley of mesquite and sagebrush. A river meandered through the flat center, and the opposite side rose in another mesa, carved with canyons. She squinted toward the east. It must have been east because the sun had begun to set behind her. There he was!

In the faraway distance, she spied the figure of a man on horseback with another pony following. It had to be McCloud. Sandra raised her hands above her head to wave. She tried calling out, but her voice was a dry croak. He probably couldn't hear her from this distance, anyway.

McCloud and his two ponies disappeared into a canyon on the opposite side of the valley.

Sandra snapped the reins and urged, "Let's go, Pansy."

The black-maned mare tossed its narrow head with more spirit than Sandra had seen since she mounted the beast. Then the animal balked. Four hooves stuck like glue on the level ridge of a gravel hillside. Pansy wasn't moving...not even when Sandra nudged with her heels and clucked her tongue against her teeth.

"Please, Pansy. Be a good girl, okay? Cooperate."

The horse snorted.

Sandra snorted right back. Her voice lost the gentle cajoling tone. "I've had it with you, nag face. Now you can move your horsey butt or I'll..."

She'd what? Throw a tantrum? Sue the beast? Apparently, Pansy had reached the end of an invisible tether, a twenty-mile leash that attached to the McCloud ranch.

Grumbling, Sandra dismounted. When her Frye boots hit the ground, her legs almost crumpled beneath her. Though she swam three times a week at the Athletic Club, her muscles weren't accustomed to riding. She leaned against the rock-solid flank of the mare and cursed McCloud. This was his fault!

She was a dusty, dirty mess. Her designer Levi's were limp. Her royal blue cotton shirt and unstructured beige jacket felt heavy with trail dust. But she wasn't going to give up. Not now. Not when she had her quarry in sight. She staggered along the edge of the mesa, dragging at the reins. Pansy shuffled contentedly behind her.

Slowly they descended the steep hillside, picking their way through scraggly piñons and clumps of mesquite. At the bottom of the hills, she was tempted to remount, but the idea of flinging her leg up and over that wide equine back was almost as painful as walking. She trudged onward, encouraged by the rippling whisper of the river. Sandra was thirsty. Hours ago, she'd consumed her only canteen of water.

Pansy seemed equally excited about the prospect of taking a long, cool drink. As they neared the river, the horse sauntered at a more motivated pace, pulling Sandra clumsily in her wake.

"Whoa," Sandra shouted. "I said whoa, you monster."

The reins ripped through her ungloved hands as Pansy cantered the last few yards. The horse stalked through the low grasses at riverside, lowered her head and slopped noisily at the water.

Making sure that she was upstream of Pansy, Sandra prepared to do likewise. The water, rushing and clear, looked delicious. She tried to squat, but her legs weren't working properly. Her knees gave out and she toppled.

Sprawled flat, she scooped out a handful of icy water, run off from the San Juans. It was wonderfully refreshing, better than a chilled Perrier with a lime twist.

After splashing her face, she took another handful. A tiny breeze spun through the straight blond hair that fell across her damp cheeks. As long as she didn't move, Sandra felt pretty darn good.

She turned her head and met Pansy's sloe-eyed gaze. The horse slowly batted its long eyelashes. If such an ignorant beast had been capable of thought, Sandra would have sworn that Pansy was plotting something. A big hoof plunked down in the river that was really little more than a wide stream. Another hoof followed.

"No," Sandra said. "Pansy, don't you dare!"

All four feet were now in the water. Another step. The horse was knee-deep.

"Stop." Sandra lunged, grabbed for the reins.

But Pansy was suddenly swift. With a grace that had been hitherto absent, the horse leapt toward the opposite bank and galloped off.

Sandra floundered in the river, drenching herself to the armpits, ruining her jacket. Cold. Ice-cold. She bolted upright. The frigid water swirled around her thighs. She plunged toward the opposite side. "Pansy! Pansy, come back!"

Charging through a bramble bush, Sandra saw the horse, standing docile and calm. Then she saw the man holding Pansy's reins. He was tall and lean and wore a black Stetson. McCloud.

She scrambled to her feet. Her mouth gaped open and closed like a fish out of water. Which was exactly how she felt. A misplaced lawyer who had been dropped in the middle of an utterly desolate landscape, in a land where torts and writs meant nothing. She shuddered as the icy damp seeped through her jeans and chapped her thighs. This wasn't fair. Especially not when she took a good hard look at McCloud. Though he hadn't seemed out of place on her turf, in the city streets of Denver, it was obvious that this land was his home. His chiseled features, his lanky form and his dusky complexion seemed a part of mesas and brush. His shirt was a faded blue, and he wore a leather vest. His Levi's were tucked into calf-high fringed moccasins. He looked strong, silent and one hundred times more masculine than the lawyers in three-piece suits whom she met every day at work.

Though she hadn't forgotten her initial attraction to him, Sandra was so outraged by his contract with her parents that she hadn't expected to find him appealing. Unfortunately, she was dead wrong about that. Much to her chagrin, she felt a flutter near her heart.

"You've been following me," he said.

All my life, she wanted to reply. Instead, she cleared her throat and tried to gather her wits, which had scattered like tumbleweed in a high wind. "I've been looking for you, McCloud. It's about time that you noticed."

"Wasn't hard. You don't exactly blend right in."

"No?"

"You're an exotic bird, Sandra. Not a dull scratchy desert hen."

Frustrated, she wished he wasn't a schemer searching for buried treasure. "Why didn't you return my calls?"

"I wanted to see you." He gestured grandly to the high plains terrain as if he owned the landscape as far as the eye could see. "On my terms."

"Choose any venue you want, McCloud. Because we have business to discuss and I'm not backing down until it is concluded to my satisfaction."

He tipped back the brim of his cowboy hat, revealing those devastating turquoise eyes. "Business?"

"Fraud," she blurted.

"You know, Sandra, that sounds like a threat."

"You're darn right, it is. And I'm perfectly capable of carrying through on it. I will prosecute." His eyes were twinkling, actually sparkling, and his full lips curved in a grin. "What's so funny, McCloud?"

"It's hard to take a wet lawyer seriously. Especially one who lost her mount and hasn't got the sense to wear a hat or gloves when she's riding. Bet you got yourself some calluses."

Not on her hands, but her bottom definitely felt bruised. "I might not be carrying my attaché case, but I am capable of handling this matter. Now, about the investment—"

"How'd you convince Pablo to let you take Pansy?"

"Pablo? The stablehand?"

"He's more than a hand. Practically runs the day-to-day operations, but he usually pulls a *no com-*

prendo routine when he doesn't want to do something, and I don't imagine he was enthusiastic about letting you use the horse.''

"I speak Spanish. And I paid him fifty dollars to rent Pansy for the afternoon.''

"Pansy belongs to me. Not Pablo.''

"That's not something I'd brag about. In my opinion, Pansy is not an example of fine horseflesh.''

"And I guess you're an expert on that, too.''

Sandra knew she'd botched this encounter so thoroughly that he was practically laughing in her face. Out here, on the plains, he had the advantage. Determinedly, she continued, "I've brought a release form with me. I'm willing to let you out of this contract without suing for damages.''

"Generous," he said wryly.

"You're darn right. Now, let me get the form from my saddle bag, you can sign and I'll be on my way.''

She reached for Pansy's reins, but before she caught hold of them, he'd snatched them up and tied them off. He slapped the horse's wide rump. "Home, Pansy.''

"Whoa!'' Sandra took a few halting steps after the horse whose easy gait had already carried her beyond reach. "Pansy, you flea-bitten, dung-dropping bag of oats. I said, whoa!''

Without looking back, the horse galloped off and disappeared behind a clump of cottonwoods. Sandra wheeled around to confront McCloud. "What the hell do you think you're doing?''

"Sending my horse back to my ranch. No law against that, is there?''

"What about me?'' She shouted, "How will I get back without a horse?''

"You could walk."

"But it's miles! And I'm tired and wet."

"Yes, you are."

Slowly his gaze surveyed every dripping inch of her body, lingering at her hips and thighs where her denim jeans clung like paint on canvas. When his careful scrutiny ascended her body, Sandra folded her arms over her breasts. Her nipples were taut, and she was infinitely glad that her upper body was well hidden beneath her soggy jacket.

Without offering a word of explanation, he turned his back on her and strode along a dusty path that wended toward the mouth of the canyon where she'd earlier sighted him and his ponies. Two ponies, she remembered. She could take one of them. She could still get away from here.

Her legs felt limp as cooked linguine, but her anger gave her strength. She stumbled after him. "Wait up, McCloud."

He didn't even slow down. Some gallantry! Wasn't there some law of the Old West that said the menfolk were supposed to care for the womenfolk? Marshal Matt Dillon would never have treated Miss Kitty this way.

Sandra forced herself onward. She was wet, tired and hungry. The last thing in the world she wanted to do was ask McCloud for help, but she had no choice. She had to borrow one of his horses. There was no way she could walk all the way back to her rental car at his ranch. Even riding wasn't a great alternative. Sandra didn't know if she could retrace her route and find his ranch. Maybe there was a highway, a town, another ranch.... But even if she did somehow manage to locate someone who might help her, she didn't have her wallet with cash and credit cards. Her purse was neatly stashed in Pansy's saddlebag.

She really was stuck here. On his terms. He'd arranged her situation as a neat little trap, and his success infuriated her. At the mouth of the canyon, Sandra plunked herself down on a smooth adobe-colored rock.

McCloud doubled back toward her. "I wouldn't do that."

"Do what?"

"Wouldn't sit down. It's going to be real hard for you to stand up again."

"That's my problem," she grumbled. "Just leave me alone."

"Suit yourself." He strode a few paces away from her.

"McCloud?"

He turned.

She snapped, "I don't need your advice."

"Stubborn." This woman was so damned stubborn. He looked beyond her to the west where a hot gold sun lowered behind the snow-capped peaks of the San Juans. She was blind, too. Apparently, she couldn't see how the red glow colored the sky and turned the clouds pink, causing the valley to seem magical, unreal. Each shrub was magnified by shadow. Glimpses of the river shone like liquid gold.

This land was special, but not everyone could experience the beauty. The farmers cursed the arid soil. Tourists raced through here on their way to somewhere else. And a lawyer like Sandra? She looked pretty angry as she picked at the tangles in her blond hair and shivered under that soggy jacket that covered the lift of her breasts.

Still, he liked her better this way than he had in the city when she'd been poised and perfectly put together. That facade was pretty, but not real. When she played the role of professional lady lawyer, he had to look deeply to find the special aura he sensed within her.

"Sandra, how did you find me?"

"Pablo gave me directions. He said to cross the road and go east until I found a river valley. You'd been out here since Tuesday, he said, exploring in canyons. So I took the high ground opposite and kept looking."

"Amazing." She had no idea of what she'd accomplished. The odds against locating him, even for an experienced tracker, were huge. Though he was pleased that she was here, he hadn't been expecting her and hadn't left an obvious trail. Yet this city woman— with no hat, no gloves and no common sense about survival—had found him in a matter of hours. "Are you always this lucky?"

"Lucky? My bottom is sore, and my clothes are wet. This jacket is ruined. I don't exactly feel like I've won the lottery."

"Pablo shouldn't have sent you out here alone."

"It wasn't his fault. I insisted."

"True." And Pablo must have figured she'd be safe on Pansy. Come sundown, that horse had a homing sense like radar. If Sandra had mounted up after drinking in the stream, Pansy would've carried her back to the ranch—whether she wanted to go there or not. "But I'm still sorry."

"You should be." Her brown eyes snapped with hostility.

"Before you sue me," he teased, "how about a cup of coffee?"

"Fine."

When she gamely staggered upright, he could see her legs trembling beneath her wet Levi's.

McCloud led the way to his makeshift camp, nestled against the canyon wall and surrounded on the other three sides by sage. A tin coffeepot perked on a small propane stove.

Sandra tumbled the last few yards. Her legs buckled, and she sank down on the dirt, propping her back against a rock. She'd never been so uncomfortable. The aroma of fresh coffee was the only thing keeping her from bursting into tears.

McCloud served her first.

She sipped from a metal cup, holding the hot liquid on her tongue and warming the inside of her mouth. Another swallow heated her throat. Closing her eyes, she savored the coffee. She wished the small cup were as big as a lake, a steaming coffee hot springs where she would wallow and bathe and soak away her stiffness.

She felt a rough heavy blanket being draped around her shoulders. Snuggling into its folds, she said, "Thank you."

He barely nodded in acknowledgment. With his own metal cup cradled in his hands, he sat cross-legged opposite her. There was a stillness about him, a calm that rose from the arid soil beneath his moccasins and permeated his lean body. He was as much a part of this land as the mesquite and piñon. If it weren't for his shocking blue eyes, she would have thought his features and manner suggested a Native American heritage.

She stirred beneath her blanket, trying to find the least painful position. "We should be going soon," she said.

"Not tonight."

"But I have to. If I drive to Alamosa tonight, I can catch a plane back to Denver first thing tomorrow morning."

"Why is it so important to get back to Denver?"

"My work," she said simply.

"Forget it, Sandra. The trail is still going to be there tomorrow." He stood and stretched. "Your torts and subpoenas will have to wait."

"That's not acceptable. I would prefer—"

His voice was firm, without a hint of teasing. "We're not going anywhere tonight."

He strode away from her to a spot where his ponies were grazing on the sparse clumps of buffalo grass. Their saddles, she noticed, had already been removed, arranged in a neat pile. McCloud dug into his saddlebags, pulled out a skillet and a couple of unidentifiable packages and cans.

Despite her outrage, his natural ease impressed her. Every motion was calm and purposeful with no wasted effort. Camping under the stars wasn't an excursion for him. It was a way of life—solitary and rugged. For over a hundred and fifty years, prospectors had wandered these very canyons, seeking a rich vein of precious metal, just as he sought his city of gold.

McCloud placed a pot on the propane stove and came back to sit beside her. Again, she launched her protest. "I must insist that you take me back to the ranch. Without the paperwork, there's no reason for me to be here."

"And what makes you think I'd sign your precious release form?"

"You'd be a fool not to. In the first place, there are dozens of loopholes that I could use to declare the contract you made with my parents null and void. You've done no due diligence. You have no collateral."

He nodded calmly. "But I do have the trust of your parents."

"Trust is not legally binding."

"And morally? If your parents want for me to use their money, why should you object?"

"Part of the investment is in my name. One hundred thousand dollars' worth."

"And that makes you unhappy."

"Unhappy?" she said suspiciously. "What do you mean?"

"Discontent. Upset. Hurt. Sorrowful."

"I'd hardly say that I'm in mourning about this ridiculous gentleman's agreement you have with my parents." He was leading somewhere, and she sensed it. McCloud was clever. A good con man always was. "My emotional well-being is unimportant."

"Being a lawyer," he said. "Does that always make you happy?"

"*Always* is a prejudicial term. Nothing in life is constant."

"I beg to differ, Counselor. The sun *always* rises in the east and sets in the west. These rocks and mountains may shift a few inches, but they're not going to change very much."

"I meant *always* as it applies to human transactions."

"Love can last forever, Sandra. *Always*. It can be as constant as the sun and the moon."

"That's not my experience," she said. The sort of love Sandra viewed most often involved commitments gone bad, trusts betrayed. Though her specialty was corporate law, not divorce, there were many family businesses that dissolved with hatred where there once had been love. "As an attorney, I don't often come in contact with love everlasting."

"Maybe you're in the wrong business."

How dare he make presumptions about her life! She was successful. Her life was arranged, complete. And she sure as heck didn't need advice from a cowboy philosopher with a treasure map in his back pocket.

And yet, when he reached toward her and the back of his fingers caressed her cheek, pushing her hair from her face, she didn't slap his hand away. She should have recoiled, should have moved away from him. And yet . . .

"Have you ever been in love, Sandra?"

Her brain felt numb. Why was he asking her these questions? What was he trying to do? "I don't want to talk about love."

He continued to stroke her face, cupped her chin and brought her gaze level with his own. The turquoise of his eyes overwhelmed her, and he said, "What about dreams? Have you ever had a dream that was so real you could touch it?"

Her body ached, yet there was a vibrance, a burning core of vitality that urged her, inch by inch, nearer to McCloud. If this moment had been a dream, she would have melted into his arms. But this was reality, and she couldn't allow him to dissuade her from her agenda.

"What about dreams, Sandra?"

"Like El Dorado? Is that a dream?"

He nodded. "Since childhood I've heard stories of the golden cities. I've dreamed about them, imagined their golden turrets reaching toward the sun. A beautiful dream.''

"A cruel dream," she contradicted. She lifted her chin and looked away from his seductive gaze.

"Why cruel?"

Sandra had done her research on his quest. "In the 1540s and 1550s, the explorer, Coronado, went looking for the Seven Cities of Cibola. In the course of his quest, he enslaved the indigenous Native American Tribes. Similarly, in Mexico, the Spaniards wiped out centuries of Aztec civilization in their greed to find cities of gold. Isn't that correct?''

"Greed was why they failed.''

"But you expect to succeed?" She glanced back toward him.

"I always get what I want.''

She should have protested his arrogance, should have pushed him away with all her strength and demanded that he take her back to his ranch at once. But he moved even closer to her. His body heat seemed to penetrate the layers of her wet clothing and warm her skin. "What are you doing, McCloud?''

"I'm going to kiss you.''

She should have objected, but desire overruled her logic. She wanted him to kiss her. Though she'd fought to suppress her fascination with his first gentle kiss on the streets of Denver, she could not. It must have been a fluke. A mistake.

His mouth slanted across hers, and pure sensation blanked her mind. No intelligible thought could break through this fierce burst of arousal. This was no soft ethereal kiss.

His arm slipped around her torso, pulling her against him. Her breasts flattened against his chest.

The blanket fell from her shoulders. Losing control, she was slipping helplessly into an unstoppable passion. She tore herself away from him. "Please, McCloud, no."

"Don't fight, Sandra. This was meant to be."

When his tongue forced her lips apart, she reveled in the quivering sensations that shot through her veins. When his grasp loosened, a moan escaped her.

He lowered her gently to the ground. Her jacket and the blanket separated her from hard rocky soil that felt soft as down pillows in her crazily aroused state. Beyond his shoulder, she saw the first pinprick light of the evening stars, an eternal glimmer from billions of miles away. Yet in that moment she felt that the light was shining just for her. The night belonged to her. And to McCloud.

She licked her lips. Her tongue still held the flavor of his kiss.

"You know, Sandra, your clothes would dry more quickly if you took them off."

Chapter Three

"Take off my clothes?" Sandra struggled to a sitting posture, pushing him away from her. Why had she ever allowed him to kiss her? Why? Temporary insanity, she thought. That was the only defense. She caught her breath and glared at him. "What do you mean, I should take off my clothes?"

"Just what I said." McCloud took off his hat, sat back on his heels, and watched her. "You can't be comfortable in that wet stuff."

She clutched at the throat of her cotton blouse. The fabric, momentarily warmed by their joined body heat, left a dank chill against her skin, and her Levi's clung heavy and sodden. Logically, he was right. She ought to remove these clothes and spread them across a shrub to dry before morning in the high desert air. But she wouldn't—couldn't—strip.

His voice rumbled, low and seductive. "You don't need to be afraid of me, Sandra."

"I'm not." She was afraid of herself, her devastating lack of willpower. Her nerves jangled. Her body craved his touch. With more assertiveness than she felt, Sandra stated, "I can handle myself. And I'll thank you, McCloud, to keep away from me."

"No promises."

"Well, of course not. You've spent all week dodging my phone calls. You took my parents' life savings. Damn you, McCloud, you chased my horse back to the ranch and stranded me here. Why should I expect you to behave like a gentleman?"

"I might," he drawled, "when you start acting like a lady."

"I've always found ladylike behavior to be a singular waste of time. There aren't many successful attorneys who follow the finer points of etiquette."

He picked up his black hat, stuck it on his head and sauntered toward the propane stove where the pot had begun to emit a fragrant steam. Calmly he hunkered down, placed a long spoon into the pot and stirred.

"You're correct," she admitted. "Catching double pneumonia would be impractical. Do you happen to have an extra shirt in those saddlebags?"

"Yep."

He moved like a shadow through the dusk. His footsteps, in the fringed moccasins, were silent. This was his land. These were his terms, and she hated herself for falling into this trap.

When he returned with a flannel shirt, she'd undone the stiff fabric around the buttons, and she tried to cock her leg to remove her wet leather boots. Her thigh muscles cramped. Her calves trembled. Every movement was agony.

He tossed her the shirt. "Thanks, McCloud. Now, how about some pants?"

"All I've got is what I have on."

"But you've been out here since Tuesday."

"I wasn't expecting company."

"Yuck! Only a man could stand to wear the same clothes for four days." His face was shadowed by the brim of his hat, but she remembered his cheeks were smooth. "At least you've been shaving. And brushing your teeth?"

"I even floss."

She made another futile attempt to grapple with her boots, but her sore muscles ached so much that her legs felt numb.

"Let me get your boots, Sandra."

Her mental debate lasted about two seconds. Though it was madness to invite him to touch her again, she was too stiff to undress herself. "Okay, McCloud. Just the boots."

He knelt beside her and gently extended her leg. The heel of her Frye boot looked small in his hand, and she felt his strength as he tugged at the leather that had molded to her swollen foot and wet sock. With a yank, the boot was off. Then the other.

She groaned with relief and slowly wiggled her toes. "Oh, my, that feels like heaven."

"It'll hurt tomorrow, putting them back on."

She sighed again, not wanting to borrow fresh pain from tomorrow when she had plenty of regrets for today. "Is that why cowboys never take their boots off? Dying with their boots on?"

"And making love. Which is hell on the sheets." He laughed. "That's why I wear moccasins."

He peeled off her once-white sock and lightly stroked her pale arch. Again, she should have told him to stop. But his foot massage was sheer bliss. Her legs sprawled helplessly as he gently kneaded the sides of her foot, flexed her ankle, worked the kinks from her toes.

"Now the pants," he said.

"Not a chance." She jolted back to her senses. Stroking her toes was one thing, taking off her pants was quite another.

"You're stiff. You're sore. Fighting with wet Levi's isn't going to be easy." He reached for the button fly at her waist. "Lie down, Sandra."

Her dubious gaze locked with his. Through the dusk, she saw a flicker of amusement in his eyes.

"I won't take advantage...unless you want me to."

"Rest assured that I don't."

She stretched back, propping herself up on her elbows to observe him through narrowed eyes, as his large hands skillfully popped open the buttons on her Levi's, one by one. When his hands accidentally brushed the soft flesh above her bikini panties, she shivered. How could she be so miserable and so turned on at the same time?

He yanked her knees up to wriggle the denim off her buttocks and she fell back to the ground with a thud. "Ouch! Be careful, McCloud. I'm not a sack of potatoes."

"You sure as hell aren't."

Through the dim light, before the moon had risen, she caught him staring at her black silk panties. Her exposed white flesh seemed to glow against the silk, and there was something irresistible about the way he was looking at her. She needed to nip these feelings in the bud. "McCloud? My Levi's?"

"Yes, ma'am. You bet."

His voice was hoarse, rough at the edges, and he didn't look at her again while he worked the wet Levi's past her knees and down her calves. He shook them once to straighten the legs and tossed them over a nearby clump of mesquite. Then he returned to his stove.

Sandra slipped off her wet shirt and put on the red flannel one he'd brought from his saddlebag. Though taking off her clothing had been dangerous in one sense, she was glad that she'd done so. Wrapped in the blanket and the shirt, she felt warmed against the night breeze that carried a definite chill.

"McCloud? Are we going to have a fire?"

"No fire."

He dished the food onto a plate and handed one to her. Sandra balanced it on her knees. The lumpy reddish-brown mess on her plate smelled spicy as she stirred it with her fork. "Is this some kind of stew?"

"Chili. Canned beans, corn, onions and dried buffalo meat."

It didn't sound appetizing, but she was hungry enough to eat fried dirt. Greedily, she cleaned her plate and set it upon the ground beside her. Her belly was full. Her body was warm. And she held a fresh cup of coffee. With a contented sigh, Sandra leaned against the tall rock behind her.

In the bustle of her life, she often forgot the simple pleasures that her parents had emphasized while she was growing up. Moments like this were a reminder. She gazed skyward. Darkness had settled around them in a thick gloom broken only by moonlight and the distant shimmer of a billion stars.

So beautiful. So peaceful. She had to remind herself that the only reason she was here was to regain her parents' investment, including the hundred thousand dollars they'd put in her name. A small shiver went through her. "Why can't we have a fire?"

"I don't want to advertise my position. You don't believe in my search, but other people do. I don't like to make it easy for them to follow my progress."

"Who is after you?"

"Outlaws."

"Oh, puh-leeze, McCloud." Her voice oozed with sarcasm. "Are we expecting Butch Cassidy and the Sundance Kid?"

"In a city, I guess, you'd call them gangs. Out here, they're tough *hombres,* renegades and trouble-makers. Some people say they're drug runners who transport the stuff from Mexico."

Sandra could believe in the existence of drug runners and troublemakers. "But why are they after you?"

"For the gold."

"El Dorado?" She rolled her eyes. Apparently, McCloud wasn't the only lunatic in this county. "If it's so dangerous, what about the sheriff?"

"Good idea, Sandra." It was his turn for sarcasm. "Maybe I can call 911 and get some help."

"Have you actually seen these bad guys?"

"Not for months."

"Well, then," she concluded, "a fire isn't really that great a risk, is it?"

"Possibly not." He shrugged. This close to his ranch, the danger of attack by the outlaw gangs who roamed these plains was minimal. "But if we have a fire, we'll probably also be visited by the Utes or Navajo. They keep an eye on me even though I've told them that if I find the city of gold, I won't destroy what might be a sacred site."

She remembered the letter from her father. "Are you an archaeologist?"

"I don't have a degree, but I've done a lot of study. Archaeology fascinates me. It's more intense than a hobby. You could even say it's an obsession."

She recalled his earlier comments. "Or a dream?"

Her insight pleased him. Now that she was physically content, her voice had lowered to a soothing alto instead of that strident lawyerly tone. Peering through the night, he wanted to see her more clearly. "Maybe we should have a fire. Even if there are outlaws around, I haven't got much worth stealing."

Leaving her in the darkness, he made ready for the night by washing their plates in the stream, checking the horses and finding dried wood. When he returned to where Sandra was sitting, he placed rocks in a circle for a small campfire.

He was aware of her gaze, her watchful eyes, and he figured she was up to something, planning a new attack.

"Tell me this, McCloud. How long have you been chasing around the countryside on this quest?"

"Off and on for nearly eight years."

"Do you have any proof whatsoever that this city of gold actually exists?"

"There's a legend," he said. "Actually several legends that are part of the lore of Navajo, Apache and Ute. The origin of these stories might have come from the Anasazi."

"But the Anasazi are an extinct tribe."

"A vanished tribe," he corrected. "There's a difference. I believe they were assimilated into other tribes, that their civilization—rather than being lost—is a part of many Native American cultures. They all have versions of the legend."

"All right, tell me the story."

"It doesn't have a neat beginning, middle and end. The logic is circular, rather than linear. I heard much of this tale from an old man I met at the ranch. His name, he told me, was Thomas Sweetwater. His face was carved like ancient driftwood, but his hair had not whitened. His long braids were black as a raven's wing."

While Sandra listened and McCloud nursed their campfire, he told of that warm day nearly ten years ago. He'd been riding the ranges, checking on the spring foals among his buffalo herd. It had been nearly noontime and McCloud had paused at a stream to drink and fill his canteen.

When he looked up from the water, Thomas Sweetwater had been standing there, still as the earth. They exchanged greetings and McCloud invited the old man to share his lunch.

After they'd eaten, Sweetwater rolled a cigarette and began to speak slowly.

Though this was not a land for cities but for tribes, there had once been a golden city. Very long ago when bear and buffalo and puma had ruled the land, man was a fragile creature with no fur to protect him in winter and no shelter to block the rage of the summer sun. Though the corn and game were plentiful, the offspring of the people were dying.

At night the warriors danced and prayed at their fires. By daylight, they buried their dead. Angered, they believed themselves cursed by another tribe and so prepared for war.

On a full moon night, a woman from the tribe came to the men. Though she was the most beautiful and the strongest among all the women, she had refused all suitors who longed for her.

She told the men that war was no answer. Instead, they must build, seeking shelter so that they might harvest the corn maize in peace. The death of the children was a warning, she said. And winter would be the death of them all.

The warriors dismissed her as being foolish. How could she say they were not good protectors? There was enough bread and meat to fill every belly. The fault was not with them. It was a curse, and they would fight to end it.

This woman, who was known as Dawn Fire, warned them three times. One man who secretly loved her listened. He went to her in the night and they made love.

The next morning, she was gone. And he hated her for leaving.

While the warriors went to fight, the women and children searched for Dawn Fire. They found her in a land where high walls touched the skies and sweet berries grew wild and profuse.

Their golden city rose magically from stone. Their children recovered from their maladies. They were safe from hunger and enemies for as long as the winds might blow and the grasses grew thick by the big river.

With the coming of winter, the man who loved Dawn Fire repented his stubbornness. He searched to the point of exhaustion, but could not find her until, one night, she came to him in a vision of fire and led him to the city of gold where they raised seven sons. Each child went forth to build his own residence in the seven cities of gold.

To this day, none have been found.

McCloud gazed through the firelight at Sandra. "According to Thomas Sweetwater, the time had come to search again. Now there is great strife on the land."

"What strife?"

"Take your pick, Sandra. Environmental. Geo-political. Economic. The world is in a time of flux."

"Am I to believe that this old Indian gentleman, this Thomas Sweetwater, referred to this strife?"

"Believe what you want." He shrugged. "What's the capital of Austria?"

"Vienna."

"And Switzerland?"

"Bern. McCloud, I don't want to play—"

"And Latvia."

"I don't know. I don't even know if Latvia is Lat-via anymore." She got the point. When she thought of the changing map of Europe, she could not deny that this was a time of strife. "I'm not denying that we live in troubled times. But I don't believe that has any-thing to do with finding a city of gold."

"There are other indications," he said. "What happened to those vanished tribes, like the Anasazi? We know they existed because of the jewelry and pot-tery from hundreds of years ago. But where did they go? And, of course, there are the Spanish stories that inspired Coronado to scour the Southwest in the mid-1500s for El Dorado."

"But no hard evidence?"

"No maps, except for the travels of Coronado, and it's my opinion that he failed to find El Dorado be-cause he got sidetracked at Cibola in New Mexico. He didn't come far enough north. At least that was one of the reasons."

"And what were the other reasons?"

"The Spaniards were motivated by greed. In the legends, the man who found Dawn Fire was moti-vated by love."

"And what motivates you?"

"Curiosity. The dream." He wanted to say more, a lot more. He wanted to assure her that he would not allow stubbornness to stand between them. "The only consistent feature in all these legends is the presence of a strong, beautiful woman. She seems to be key in the search."

Sandra drew her arms back from the fire and hugged the warmth to her body. There was something about the way McCloud was watching her that made her distinctly uncomfortable. "If this woman is the key to your search, why are you out here alone?"

"I'm not alone. Not right now."

The flickering glow lit her face, and he was glad that he'd risked building a fire. Watching her gave him immense pleasure. Her wide brown eyes, the way she tilted her head when she was thinking, even the tangles in her hair. Did she know how lovely she was? He doubted it. Sandra was beauty unaware. Now that she was here with him, he knew that his quest was almost at an end.

"I'm not alone," he repeated. "You're here with me."

"McCloud, I sincerely hope that you aren't implying that I'm this woman, this Dawn Fire."

"You found me out here. The odds against that are astronomical. You can't dismiss that."

"A coincidental stroke of luck doesn't mean I'm the twentieth-century embodiment of an Anasazi legend."

She tucked the edges of the blanket around her legs. His story about Dawn Fire intrigued her, but she interpreted Thomas Sweetwater's message in a less literal sense. The idea that a woman would lead her people to a safer, more productive life seemed like a fitting metaphor for a time of strife. But as proof? As a factual indication that a city of gold existed? She simply could not accept a legend as evidence.

But she was too tired to spar with him about proof and fantasy. All she wanted was for him to sign the release form, return her parents' money and she'd leave him to his legends and his quest.

In the distance, a coyote howled and she had to suppress a shiver. It was so strange that out here, where there were probably no humans for miles and miles, she felt like she was being observed, as if hundreds of silent eyes were watching them. She felt a need for shelter in the night. "Are you going to pitch a tent?"

"Would you like that?"

"Yes."

"It's only a little pup tent."

"Please."

In a moment, he'd gone to his saddlebags and knapsacks, finding a plastic sack only slightly larger than a couple of bread loaves. With a few twists of aluminum poles and hammering stakes and weaving ropes through grommets, he'd set up a small bright blue pup tent.

"Very modern," she approved.

"I only carry this in case of rain," he said. "Usually I prefer the stars overhead."

"Now all I need is a sleeping bag."

"I only carry one bedroll." In the firelight, she saw him smile. "I guess we'll have to share."

"No way, McCloud." A surge of panic twisted in her chest. Share a sleeping bag? Immediately, she flashed on an image of him lying beside her, holding her, making love to her. A dangerous image.

Before she could announce her arguments, he'd returned to his equipment. He unzipped the bag and spread it on the floor on the tent. "I'll be a gentleman," he said. "You take the tent and the bag."

"Very gallant," she said, "especially since I wouldn't be stranded here in the first place if it weren't for you."

On her stiff aching legs, Sandra crawled into the pup tent and snuggled into the down sleeping bag. The scent she'd come to identify with McCloud permeated the lining, and she inhaled deeply of the masculine fragrance. He had to be the sexiest man she'd ever encountered. But dreamers always were. The Don Quixotes of the world were the men who inspired fantasies, but made disastrous partners.

"Dawn Fire," she mumbled. For a moment, he had actually seemed to believe that she was a reincarnated princess of a vanished tribe. Ridiculous! Sandra wasn't a dreamer. She embraced the ongoing complexities of the real world. As an attorney, she worked hard to make real life bearable.

She slept fitfully on the hard earth and wakened to the sound of voices. It was still quite dark. Sandra lay still and listened, but the words were unintelligible, somehow garbled. Moving as quietly as possible on her sore muscles, she peeked through the slit at the front of the tent.

McCloud had company at the small campfire. Two solidly built men sat with their backs to her. They were all speaking in a language she did not understand.

Compelled by an urge she did not fully comprehend, Sandra pushed aside the tent flap. With the lower half of her body wrapped in the striped blanket, she stepped into the firelight. "What's going on, McCloud?"

"Sandra Carberry, I'd like to introduce Martin White Horse and Hank Broken Wing."

The two men stood politely and nodded their heads. Hank Broken Wing, the younger of the two said, "Sorry we disturbed you, miss. Martin and I noticed McCloud's fire and we took this opportunity to catch up on his progress."

Martin White Horse studied her with intent speculation. His lined face was dark, making sharp contrast with his long white hair which he wore in a tight bun at the nape of his neck. His moccasins were similar to McCloud's, but the fringe was knotted with silver and turquoise beads. His belt buckle showed an ornate silver eagle. And the shirt he wore beneath a heavy leather jacket was homespun material.

His expression, highlighted by the firelight, seemed stern and forbidding. He stuck out a huge paw. "Sandra Carberry. You work for Jessop, Feldner and White."

It would not have been more shocking if he'd burst into a medley of show tunes. Gaping, Sandra grasped his hand. "Yessir, I do."

"I have noticed you," Martin said. "Your firm is handling an important case for the Navajo and Ute nations, involving water rights. We have been working with Maxwell Teller."

"Small world," she said.

Though it was truly astonishing to encounter a client in the middle of a desert, it was no surprise that Jessop, Feldner and White were involved in an environmental lawsuit. Their admirable stand on those issues was one of the reasons Sandra had joined the firm in the first place.

"What is your opinion of Teller?" Hank asked.

She'd been an attorney long enough to know how to hide her personal dislike for Max the Ax with diplomacy. "He has an excellent record," she said honestly. "He's a ruthless competitor. And I understand that he plays a great game of golf."

While they exchanged pleasantries, Sandra was struck by the utter incongruity of making small talk about golf scores while standing around a campfire in this land of mystery and desolate legend.

When Hank and Martin left, disappearing into the night, she listened to the whinny of their horses, then turned to McCloud with wide eyes. "Am I dreaming?"

"Your father might say that all of life is a dream."

"My father is a charming eccentric." Sandra sank down in the place she'd sat before and leaned toward the waning fire.

"Some people might say he's a visionary. A genius."

"And others, myself included, might say he was easily duped." She looked up at him sharply. She wanted this settled. Now! "You took advantage of him, McCloud. You dazzled him with your legends and your schemes, and he gave you his life savings."

"Only for two years' time. Then I'll return his money. And his investment will become a fortune if I find the city of gold."

She cut to the heart of the matter. "When we get back to your ranch, will you sign the release form and return his money?"

"That can be arranged."

"It can?" Taken aback, she could only stare. Was he really acquiescing to her demands? "Why should I believe you?"

"You have my word."

He hunkered down beside her. In his heavy jacket, his shoulders looked broad and powerful. His Levi's outlined the muscles in his thighs. Was he really giving up without any more fight? "We could have taken care of this business on the phone."

His eyes crinkled in a smile. "But I wanted to see you."

He wanted more than that. Seeing her only utilized one of his senses. And McCloud wanted to fully experience the woman who sat with her legs stretched toward the dying embers of the fire and her back propped against a high stone.

He wanted to hear her voice, that slight huskiness after he kissed her. He wanted to inhale the fragrance of her milky smooth skin. To touch her. To taste...

"McCloud?" What was he thinking? For a moment, she wished he was someone different, someone she could easily understand. Then, perhaps, she could dismiss her absurd attraction to him. But he wasn't like any man she'd ever met. He was exotic, unique and amazingly sexy.

She watched the flicker of firelight on the sharp planes of his face, his high cheekbones. Sandra dragged herself back to the business at hand. The realities. "You're being very sensible. A court battle would have been—"

"Unnecessary. I don't want money from people who don't believe in what I'm doing."

"Well, then..." She rested the palms of her hands on her outstretched thighs. "I guess that's all we need to talk about. I'm quite surprised, actually. Most people would have fielded more objections."

"I'm not like other men."

That, she thought, was an understatement. McCloud was definitely unique, one of a kind.

"That bothers you," he said.

"What do you mean?"

"You'd be more comfortable if I was a professional man. A doctor or an accountant or a lawyer."

"That doesn't matter to me." And yet, Sandra hesitated. Her life goals, becoming a partner in the law firm, indicated a certain type of man who would be appropriate.

"For the sake of argument," he said, "would you ever consider marriage to a man like me?"

"Marriage?" she squeaked. A long-term commitment? She couldn't imagine living with McCloud in the high plains. He was an extremely unlikely partner for a woman like her.

"I didn't think so," he said. "Then answer me this, Sandra. Would you consider making love to a man like me?"

Her gaze locked with his, and the spark between them kindled into a searing flame. She couldn't deny the way he disrupted her sensibilities. In a glance, he mocked her willpower and fired an unbearable heat within her. She shouldn't respond to his question. Logic warned against being close to him, but her mouth yearned for his kiss. Her nipples were hard against the flannel shirt. Staring up, she sought answers in the heavens, in the distant pure stars overhead. At her feet, the camp fire winked down to a few shimmering embers. The heat was almost gone, and she trembled.

Without saying a word, he peeled off his jacket and spread it across the blanket that covered her outstretched legs.

Lightly, foolishly, she reached up and caressed his cheek. "You look tired, McCloud."

"I was just nodding off when Hank and Martin showed up."

Sandra knew she should take her hand away. It was imprudent to tempt the Fates that seemed to be drawing her closer to McCloud. Yet she needed to touch him, to ground herself in this confusing world where Native Americans chatted about golf scores, and dinner was buffalo-meat chili, and the walls of the canyons echoed with unspoken dreams. There was too much magic in the pure desert air, and she could almost believe that a golden city was hidden behind the next horizon.

He caught her hand in his, and she felt his strength. Her breath caught in her throat.

He knelt beside her, taking her other hand.

Sandra leaned her back against the stone. Her chin tilted upward, baring her throat to him in a feral gesture of submission. Her conscious objections faded, consumed by yearning, a desire to once again taste the sweet warmth of his kiss.

His mouth was hot. His tongue forced her lips apart, and she welcomed him. Her own tongue quested into his mouth, savoring the slick surface of his teeth.

As their kiss deepened, she struggled against the restraint of his strong hands holding hers. She longed to touch him. As soon as he released his grasp, she caressed the rock-hard muscles of his chest, kneading the fabric of his shirt, pulling him toward her.

His fierce embrace crushed her against his torso, and his mouth, still hot, bruised her lips.

She was dizzy, sliding desperately toward an uncontrolled surge of pure animal pleasure. This was insanity! There was no way she could allow herself to succumb to these desires. "McCloud. We shouldn't. We—"

"Don't speak, Sandra. For once, don't object."

"But I—"

"You want this as much as I do."

He lifted her from the ground and carried her to the tent. The blue fabric enclosed them like a cocoon. He stretched her out on the sleeping bag and she peered up at him through the darkness.

"Sandra, I said before that I wouldn't take advantage of you."

"Yes," she murmured. In the small portion of her brain that was still rational, she remembered.

"I meant it," he said. "I want to make love to you. But if you want me to go, tell me now. Do you understand?"

She nodded.

In a strong, deep voice, he said, "Tell me to stay."

There should have been dozens of reasons for her to object, but she couldn't think of a single one. Sandra's mind and body were ruled by the passions he had ignited within her. Making love with McCloud might be the biggest mistake of her life. But that was a chance she was destined to take.

Slowly and deliberately Sandra reached for the top button on her flannel shirt. "McCloud," she said, "take off your hat."

Chapter Four

There was no explanation for her behavior. No rationalization. No logic. Sandra had never allowed herself to be so easily seduced. But then...she'd never known a man like McCloud.

After their lovemaking, she'd slept soundly in his arms. It was a deep, refreshing slumber, and she wakened with a smile, knowing that her dreams had been beautiful though she could not remember the images.

Careful not to rouse McCloud, she disentangled from his embrace. Kneeling over him, she studied the planes and angles of his features from his strong jaw to the high cheekbones and the thick head of shining black hair. Even while sleeping, he looked strong and virile. Not at all vulnerable.

She crept out of the small pup tent to witness the dawn. Her gaze turned toward the west, and she watched as the shadows faded and the last twinkling stars disappeared. To the east new sunlight streaked the skies with magenta and gold. The natural splendor mesmerized her, and if she'd believed in magic, Sandra would have thought that she'd fallen under an enchanted spell.

The morning passed in a shimmering haze. She must have eaten breakfast, must have spoken to McCloud, must have dressed herself in her dried Levi's and shirt. But she was utterly unaware of the mechanics of living. Instead, her gaze would fasten on the bright flash of color in the brush—the scarlet of an Indian paintbrush, the royal purple of cactus flowers. Her ears heard new sounds, such as the hush of wind through trees and the cooing of doves.

As they packed up their camp and prepared to leave, she listened to the music in McCloud's deep baritone as he said, "Stay with me."

Had she heard him correctly? "What did you say?"

"I'd like you to stay with me at the ranch."

"What do you mean? For how long?"

"As long as you like, Sandra." His smile was lazy and satisfied. "I'd like to show you this part of the country. And at night..."

He left the promise hanging. An enticing prospect, she thought. Too readily, she imagined the excitement of making love in an actual bed with all the comforts.

It would be so easy to indulge her desire for him, to spend the rest of the week at his ranch leisurely making love every night. But that would only make it harder to leave.

"I can't," she said in a small voice.

Her life was in Denver. Her reality included monthly bills and car payments and an office that had a view of Pikes Peak on a clear day. Sandra had worked hard to attain her accomplishments, and she could not give up all her achievements to follow a crazy man with impossible dreams of El Dorado.

"Maybe just for tonight," he said.

"Maybe."

Then they mounted his ponies and rode back to his ranch.

The two hours' jostling on horseback numbed her sensuality. Her muscles still ached from the day before. No matter how she arranged her rump on the saddle, each jolt was uncomfortable. This was a dose of hard reality, with a vengeance, and Sandra was forced to abandon her idyllic sense of perfection. The gears in her brain began to mesh. She began to think, again. And to make plans and agendas.

When they paused on a small ridge overlooking his ranch, she said, "First thing, when we get there, I need to find out what happened to the things I had in Pansy's saddlebags. And then you are going to sign that release form."

"Am I?"

"Of course." She glanced up at him. He sat tall in the saddle, perfectly at ease on horseback. "You gave me your word, McCloud."

"I told you that I would give your parents' money back," he clarified. "And I always intended to do that. After two years."

Sandra couldn't believe what she was hearing. "Are you telling me that you won't sign the forms?"

"It depends upon what they say." He wouldn't look at her. His turquoise eyes, shaded beneath his black Stetson, focused on the ranch below them. "This is a fairly complicated operation."

"Not from what I've seen. It's not like you're using complicated technology, McCloud. A couple of horses and a compass can't be all that expensive. I don't know why you need so much financing, anyway."

"I'm paying for permission to search. According to Colorado law, it doesn't matter who finds a treasure. The law says that whoever owns the land, owns whatever might be found upon it."

"Don't quote law to me." She bristled.

"Fine." He nudged his horse's flank with his heels and started down the hill.

"Wait up, McCloud." She urged her mount forward a few paces. "Are you buying all this land? That's crazy! When you get done with your stupid quest, you'll be stuck with acres and acres of worthless desert."

"That's why I'm not buying it forever. I have what amounts to a two-year lease with an option to buy. In addition to the fixed fee that I pay for the privilege of searching, I place an amount—equal to the value of the land—in an escrow account. If I find the city of gold, I exercise my option to buy, the escrow money goes directly to the original landowner and the deed comes to me. Otherwise, at the end of two years, the agreement ends."

"And that's when you pay back my parents."

"Correct. And I return the property to the landowner, none the worse for wear. Most of them think it's a sweet deal."

"I see no reason why you can't return my parents' investment right now," she said. "No legal reason whatsoever."

"It's already tied up in escrow."

"Pull it out."

"But, then, I wouldn't have a lease." He pushed back the brim of his hat and looked her squarely in the eye. "Be reasonable, Sandra. I'll return the money after two years. That's guaranteed."

Reasonable? He was accusing her of being unreasonable? He'd lied to her. He'd led her to believe that he'd sign the forms. Worse than that, she'd trusted him. She'd made love to the man. "You're nothing but a cheap scam artist, McCloud. Last night you said you didn't want money from people who didn't believe in your quest."

"Your mother and father believe in me."

"Well, I don't. And one hundred thousand of their investment is in my name."

"I'll sign a release for your money, Sandra. I'll return it to you today with a check. But not the rest of it. Not until I've had my two years' worth of searching."

He clicked his heels against his horse's flank and rode swiftly down the sloping gravelly hillside toward his ranch. Sandra stayed behind, seething in the late-morning sun.

SHE NEVER SHOULD HAVE made love to him.

Four days later, Sandra scooted her swivel chair up to the desk, crossed her legs and plucked her pen from the pewter holder with Congratulations, Ms. Partner inscribed on the base. She stared at the legal brief on the desktop in front of her until the words blurred in a haze that reminded her—as everything reminded her—of the high plains desert at the foot of the San Juans.

The trail dirt had washed off easily. The aching in her buttocks and her legs had subsided. But the memories of McCloud were as vivid as if he were still making love to her.

"Dammit." He hadn't telephoned, hadn't sent a letter or a carrier pigeon with a message. He hadn't apologized, and he certainly hadn't offered to sign the release form.

Sandra dropped her pen on the desktop. A weak sigh puffed through her lips. She had every reason to despise Russel McCloud, yet each time she thought of him, her mind replayed that desert night. She'd relived her passion a million times, and the memory grew sharper with each repetition.

"Damn you, McCloud."

Her telephone buzzed on the interoffice line, and Sandra jumped. She snatched the receiver. "Yes?"

"Jessop here. I need you in Maxwell's office."

"Yessir."

A frown puckered her forehead. Confrontations in Maxwell's office were always distasteful, and her promotion to partner made it worse. She and Maxwell were the same age and had much the same experience. Max the Ax, the most vicious competitive trial lawyer in the firm, claimed that she had been invited to be partner instead of him for only one reason: Jessop, Feldner and White wanted a female partner.

She hurried down the hall. The door to Maxwell's office was closed, but his secretary nodded and Sandra stepped inside. Seated in the two plush leather chairs opposite Maxwell's desk were Hank Broken Wing and Martin White Horse. They rose when Sandra entered.

Suspicious, she smiled and shook their hands. Both men maintained a stoic calm.

Maxwell Teller, with his blond hair slicked back and his shirtsleeves rolled up, managed to look hardworking and smug at the same time. He always talked down to Sandra, as if she were a dull-witted child. "You've met my clients before."

"Yes," Sandra said, frantically struggling to suppress her memories of that night. "Last weekend I went to Alamosa to deal with a personal problem."

"Your personal life is interfering with my case," Maxwell said. "Or so it seems."

"I'll handle this." The elderly Laurence Jessop spoke in a whispery sibilant voice. An asthmatic condition had curtailed his brilliant career as a trial attorney, but his authority within the firm remained unquestioned. "Last weekend you met with Russel McCloud. Is that correct, Sandra?"

"Yessir. My parents have invested in McCloud's search for El Dorado."

"El Dorado?" Jessop took a moment to breathe. He always seemed to monitor his air supply, as if there were only so much available to him. "Martin and Hank believe this site has significance, archaeological importance, for the Ute and Navajo tribes in the southwestern corner of Colorado."

"Perhaps it does," she said. "If the site exists."

"Exactly so." Jessop nodded to Martin White Horse. "Would you explain your position to Sandra?"

"McCloud has searched for many years. He consulted with our people and recorded our legend. I believe he has spoken to you of this."

"Yes, he told me the legend of Dawn Fire."

"A most fortunate and intelligent woman." Martin White Horse smiled. "But this is not unusual. As my wife has convinced me, all women are wise."

"At least we agree on that," Sandra said.

"You, Sandra, are unusual. McCloud told us of your ability to find him with no directions in miles and miles of desert."

"Very fortunate," Hank Broken Wing put in.

"But maybe not so wise," Sandra said. She feared the direction this conversation seemed to be leading. The two Native American men, clients of Jessop, Feldner and White, were hinting that she had some connection with Dawn Fire. "I don't know why locating McCloud seems like such a big deal. You found him later that night."

"With rising smoke and a fire to lead us," said Hank.

Martin White Horse continued, "We, too, have invested in McCloud. It is our hope that he succeed in his search, and the legend says that a woman will lead him. You, Sandra, might be that woman."

Jessop stepped in. "Martin and Hank would like for you to spend some time with McCloud on his quest. And I've arranged for you to take two weeks off."

While Sandra stiffened with disbelief, the senior partner stood and shook hands with Martin and Hank. "Always good to meet with you, gentlemen."

On his way out, Martin winked at Sandra. "Your journey, Sandra, will not be unpleasant. McCloud is a good man."

The door closed behind them, and Sandra exploded. "I am not going to accompany McCloud on his crackpot search! That is a final decision."

"Not so fast." Maxwell sat behind his desk. He steepled his fingertips. "I've been working with the Navajo for two years and they've been totally cooperative."

Jessop added, "This is the first time Martin White Horse has asked for a favor."

"No."

She pivoted on her heel. Return to the buffalo ranch? Spend two weeks in the company of McCloud? It would be emotional suicide! Her fingers clenched on the doorknob.

"Wait," Jessop said.

Slowly Sandra turned. She had the distinct feeling that she wasn't going to like what he had to say.

"If you were an associate—" Jessop drew a breath. "Or an employee, I would not insist."

"But I'm a partner," she said.

"Think about that responsibility. The Navajo account not only brings in a great deal of revenue, but it is a positive identification for the firm."

"She's going to screw this up," Maxwell said. "After all the work I've put in on this case, Sandra, the firm owes it to me to appease my clients."

"I'll take them out to the golf course," she said. "I'll buy them dinner. But I am not going to deck myself out in feathers and dance around a campfire, pretending that I'm the reincarnation of some ancient Indian legend."

"Sandra!" Mr. Jessop was sharp. "This isn't a joke. Comments like that are not acceptable. Not even from a partner."

"You're right, sir. And I apologize."

He walked slowly to the door and opened it. "Pack your suitcases for a two-week stay, Sandra. You'll be leaving in the morning."

Before she could offer further objection, Mr. Jessop walked out of the office.

Maxwell leaned across his desk, smirking like the cat who swallowed the canary. "How do you like being a partner, Carberry? Pressure getting to you?"

"If you engineered this, Maxwell, I'll—"

"Hey, don't blame me. You brought this on yourself." He chuckled evilly. "Dawn Fire."

She returned to her desk and punched the long-distance phone number for McCloud. Expecting to get his answering machine, as always, she was surprised to hear his voice.

"McCloud? Is that you?"

"Sandra. I've missed you. This morning's sunrise was beautiful. I wanted to share it with you."

She remembered another sunrise...after a night of lovemaking. Facing the east, she'd watched the midnight blue thin to a delicate eggshell color, streaked with gold and pink. She'd never seen such a sunrise.

Her hand on the receiver was suddenly sweaty. A muscle twitched in her jaw. Frustrated, she blurted into the telephone receiver, "Dammit, I wish I'd never met you. I wish I could forget that I ever saw your face."

"Don't fight it, Sandra. You're a part of me. I'm a part of you."

"No," she protested, as much to herself as to him. That part of her, the part that had joined with him on a starry night, felt impossibly strong, but she fought against her natural impulse to capitulate. She could not allow her hormones to rule her life.

"Come stay with me, Sandra. For a week. Or a month."

"Oh, you're smooth, McCloud. You've pretty much insured that I'll have to stay with you. But don't make the mistake of believing that I'm a willing guest. I hate being manipulated."

"What the hell are you talking about?"

"Martin White Horse and Hank were here, at my law firm, and they made their ridiculous demand that

I join your quest because I'm the reincarnation of Dawn Fire. Now don't tell me that you had nothing to do with their visit."

He chuckled. "But I didn't."

"Then how did they know that I accomplished this allegedly fantastic feat of finding you?"

"Not fantastic," he corrected. "Just incredibly lucky."

"How did they know?"

"You know the answer to that question, Sandra. You saw me talking to Martin and Hank at the campfire."

Before she and McCloud had made love. Was he plotting, even then, to get her back to his ranch? But why? Why go to such an elaborate extreme? She wondered what exactly he had said to them. They'd been conversing in a language she didn't understand. She took a guess. "Were you speaking Navajo?"

"Yes."

"Because you didn't want me to understand what you were saying?"

"Martin and I always speak in Navajo."

"Around the campfire. Is that when you three hatched this scheme? Or was it later?"

"Don't cross-examine me, Sandra." The geniality left his voice. "I don't lie. Not ever."

"Do you deny that you knew about their visit to Jessop, Feldner and White? Do you deny that you've arranged it so I'll be forced to join you on your quest?"

"I'd never force you. That's not what I want."

"Well, McCloud, this is one time when you're not going to get exactly what you want. I'll arrive tomorrow afternoon and I will be staying for approximately two weeks. But I guarantee you, this will not be a pleasant visit."

She slammed down the receiver. In spite of her assertive telephone manner, Sandra's insides had turned to a quivering mass of jelly. Boneless and weak, she flopped back in the chair behind her desk. Placing her elbow on the armrest, she suspended her hand at eye level and observed, in an almost detached manner, as tremors vibrated through her fingers. She lowered her hand to her breast where she could feel her heart fluttering. How on earth could she expect to spend time with this man without losing control? Even a phone conversation was enough to throw her into spasms of lust.

He was probably counting on that, she thought. McCloud was arrogant enough to believe that he could charm away her anger and bend her to his whim. He thought he could romance her into forgetting about the six hundred thousand dollars. A ludicrous idea, but it made a certain horrible sense. If he was hiding an illegality, he might think she would be so besotted that she wouldn't delve any deeper into his investor's contracts.

Sandra cringed inside. That might have been why he seduced her the first time. To protect his investment scam. Maybe that was why he'd come to Denver to meet her. Not to participate in *Cinco de Mayo,* but to make contact with the lady lawyer who might know enough to throw a wrench into his plans.

What other reason could there be? The legend?

No way. McCloud hadn't been thinking of the legend when they met for the first time outside the Athletic Club. In retrospect, that evening was fuzzy and unfocused. Dancing in the streets. A fleeting kiss on a street corner. Her designer dress of virginal white. And the cocktail party where she'd been formally welcomed as a partner, the most important occasion of her professional life.

Her profession. Had accepting the partnership been a mistake? Maybe Max the Ax was right. Maybe the pressure would be too difficult. But she wouldn't give up without trying. If it was her job to appease the clients and go to McCloud's ranch, so be it.

Though she would participate in this absurd quest, Sandra had no intention of being a docile participant in her own betrayal. There were ways of fighting back, and she intended to avail herself of each one.

She buzzed her secretary. There was a lot of work to be accomplished in the next few hours. Sandra's calendar for the coming two weeks had to be cleared. And new plans needed to be made. Plans for McCloud.

As Sandra flipped through her Rolodex, a determined smile curved her lips.

Chapter Five

McCloud sat at the huge old desk in his office at the ranch, drowning in paperwork. He had to clear off the monthly accounts and prepare a written list of details for Pablo to handle during the next two weeks. Papers, papers and more papers, to be shuffled from one stack to another or to an envelope or file drawer. He wasn't in the mood for this. He yanked off his reading glasses and stared through the window at the rising blue vista of the San Juans.

Beneath the desk, his feet began to fidget. The pencil he held between forefinger and thumb drummed on the desktop. Dammit, he had an itch that needed to be scratched. And the name of that irritant, that bur under his saddle, was Sandra Carberry.

Yesterday she'd told him she'd be arriving today. Told him? *Threatened* was a more accurate description. The woman had been snarling on the phone, accusing him of setting up some kind of scheme with Martin and Hank. Crazy idea! In McCloud's experience, he'd found it nearly impossible to get Martin to agree with Hank, much less to reach consensus among the other Navajo leaders. Decisions among this group of Native Americans were not reached easily, and he'd

He pulled Guevera to a halt. If he didn't force the animal to rest, Guevera would run until he dropped from exhaustion. McCloud stroked the horse's neck. They'd stopped on the plateau that overlooked his ranch, the last place where Sandra had spoken to him in a halfway civil manner. What an impossible, complicated woman she was. As soon as she decided that he wasn't giving her exactly what she wanted, she'd turned back into Sandra, the shark attorney.

Dammit, when would she be here?

As a rule, McCloud didn't much like professionals. But he'd known from the start that she was different. Sandra was the daughter of Thornton and Emma Carberry, the little girl who had memorized the capitals of Europe.

Hell, yes, she was different. When they'd made love, McCloud had been stunned by her abandon. Her passion made control impossible, and he'd forced himself to continually pull away from her so that he wouldn't climax too quickly.

He needed to make love to her again. Slowly. He wanted to take his time, to bring her to the brink of ecstasy and to watch her face as she plummeted, uncontrolled, into the sweet abyss of pleasure that only a woman can know.

They would make love again. It was destiny.

Where was she? Why was it taking so long?

Earlier that morning, he'd tried to figure out flight schedules from Alamosa. But she might drive. Why hadn't she given him an arrival time? He could have arranged with Elena for a special candlelight dinner.

A rumbling sound disturbed the earth. Rain?

McCloud looked up into a cloudless sky.

Then he saw the helicopter.

THE HELICOPTER, a Bell Jet Ranger, hovered over the ranch, then neatly lowered, kicking up a small dust storm. Letty Sternbaum, the owner of Copter-Tours and Sandra's good friend, cut the engine and the chopper blades stilled.

Sandra pulled off the earphones and shook her head to clear the constant hum. Shoving open the helicopter door, she descended gratefully to solid ground. Though she tried to keep from gloating, she knew that her entrance had been impressive. With her fists braced on hips, she looked around for McCloud.

Pablo sauntered toward the helicopter, muttering in Spanish under his breath.

"Is McCloud here?" she asked.

"No comprendo inglés."

Sandra knew from McCloud's comments the last time she was here that Pablo spoke English very well, but she played along with him. In Spanish, she said, "I'm looking for McCloud. He is expecting me."

"And the helicopter?" Pablo asked. In English. "He's not expecting that."

"Oh, I sincerely hope not."

Pablo's scowl disappeared, and Sandra smiled back, recognizing a man who appreciated a good prank, even when the butt of the joke was his boss. Pablo's expression became even more joyful when he spied Letty, A Valkyrie-size blonde, dressed in a tailored pink jumpsuit.

"Nice place," Letty said. "I'll bet you guys could use a helicopter service for getting back and forth to civilization."

"Oh, yes," Pablo agreed. "And for rounding up the herd. Helicopters, yes."

"I'll leave you a quote," Letty promised. "Maybe a once-a-month run down here. Or another Ranger, out of Pueblo?"

Sandra appreciated Letty's newfound confidence. When they'd first met, a couple of years ago, this dynamic female pilot had been unable to go for more than ten minutes without bursting into tears. Then Sandra had arranged the divorce terms from Letty's partner in Copter-Tours. Without the deadweight of her ex-partner/ex-husband, Letty had taken off, literally.

"Would you..." Pablo stumbled on the words. "Would you teach me to fly?"

"I'm a certified instructor. So I can teach you, but I'm not cheap."

"McCloud can pay for it," Sandra said. "He seems to have money to burn. Or to throw away on goofy quests."

She stared toward the house, toward the barn. Her weight shifted from one foot to the other and back again. The anticipation she'd been denying since yesterday had risen to an almost unbearable level. "Pablo, where is he?"

He pointed toward the open plains, and she turned. The figure who approached them was hazy in the distance, a man from a dream, preparing to charge into her consciousness. Closer and closer he came, riding with easy grace on his high-spirited black mustang. Sandra again felt that she'd been bested by this cowboy. The nearer he came, the more fantastic he seemed.

He tugged on the reins, and the horse reared impressively. McCloud was not unseated, not even bothered. He was in control, handling his mount with natural mastery. His powerful thighs gripped the horse's flanks. Today he was wearing boots and, of course, his Stetson. He looked like the quintessential cowboy, a Marlboro man without the cigarettes.

Letty gaped. "Wow! That's McCloud?"

"Don't let his looks deceive you." With some effort, Sandra kept the tremble from her voice. "He's the most manipulative, conniving—"

"So what? Sandra, that cowboy can hang his lariat on my bedpost any night of the week."

Sandra dismissed the tiny bite of jealousy as she tried to keep track of all her other emotions. Primary among her myriad reactions was a fierce joy. Her pleasure at seeing him went straight to her heart, and her hand flew to her face to cover the warm blush that bloomed on her cheeks like a disobedient rose.

Instead, she concentrated on her anger, her outrage. He'd manipulated her through her work to bring her down here. He'd made love to her, had given her the most intense erotic experience of her whole life, and then... he'd tricked her, used her. Though McCloud looked like an unsophisticated buffalo rancher, he was slick. A con man.

She clung to her anger. It was the only emotion that made sense.

He dismounted in a swoop, tossed the reins to Pablo and came to her. There was no mistaking his excitement. A firm smile curved his lips. His turquoise eyes linked with hers, glancing neither left nor right. Sandra felt as if she were the only woman in the world.

He stopped just short of her, facing her. He was breathing hard after his ride. His chest rose and fell. A hint of dark chest hairs roughened the skin at his throat.

Much to his credit, he didn't presume to sweep her into his arms. But it was an impossibly awkward moment. Sandra struggled with her reaction to him. She ought to slap that grin right off his face.

"Sandra," he whispered in a low, musical voice. "I thought you'd never get here."

His words were poetry, but she couldn't allow herself to listen. She'd been seduced once. It would not happen again. "Being here," she said, "is not my choice."

His eyes silently questioned, and she continued determinedly, "You arranged for me to come here, McCloud. I don't know why. I can't possibly guess at your motives, but I want you to understand that I'm here to do a job."

His chin drew back an inch, as if she actually had slapped him. His expression cooled. "A job?"

"Yes. The Navajo leaders who came to my law firm requested that I help you in your search, and that is all I intend—"

"Help me? You're here to help me?"

"Yes." Sandra introduced Letty. "She'll be here for two days. I thought a search by helicopter would be far more time effective than riding up and down the canyons. If you'll cooperate by allowing us to see some of your maps, we can start immediately."

His anger was unmistakable, but his tone remained civil. "Certainly. Come into my office."

When he turned on his heel and strode away from her, Sandra's heart felt heavy as a brick. "McCloud," she called after him. "Should we bring our luggage?"

He shook his head and returned. "Where are your suitcases?"

They off-loaded them from the helicopter. In addition to a briefcase jammed with work from the office, Sandra had brought three huge cases, filled with every jacket and every pair of sensible shoes that she owned. If this quest actually required a march through the arroyos, she would be prepared for every kind of weather.

They entered the sprawling ranch house through the kitchen where Sandra reintroduced herself to Elena, the sturdy Hispanic woman who did the cooking for four full-time employees who worked at the ranch house and the occasional cowhands who came in from tending the herd. The last time Sandra was here, she learned that McCloud's operation was fairly simple. He raised the animals, but left the processing to a company in Pueblo.

He dropped her suitcases on the bed in a spacious bedroom with a rough heavily carved headboard on the bed. The decor had a masculine feel, as did every room in the house. The sparse furniture was heavy and functional. Wall decoration was simple, but the occasional paintings—like the landscape in this bedroom—were of exceptional quality, warmly reflecting the terra-cotta browns and beiges and turquoise colors typical of the southwestern states. Likewise, the window curtains harmonized with this soothing color scheme.

McCloud escorted Letty to the bedroom next door, and Sandra heard the helicopter pilot's exclamations of pleasure at her accommodations. Too much enthusiasm? If Letty had designs on McCloud, Sandra would... She squelched a shimmer of jealousy. Letty had no reason to believe that she was trespassing on Sandra's man. Practically everything Sandra had said about McCloud had been derogatory.

There was a bathroom between the two rooms, and the two women met there. Letty was excited. "That McCloud is a total babe. Those eyes! Those shoulders! That body! Are you sure you're not interested in him?"

Sandra splashed water in one of the two sinks. "He's nothing but trouble."

Letty folded her arms across her pink jumpsuit and perched one hip on the tiled counter. "I'll tell you, Sandra, I'm not real smart when it comes to men. If it hadn't been for your legal advice, I would have given everything to my ex-husband. But I do know one thing."

Sandra dashed water on her cheeks, then glanced up in the mirror, meeting Letty's steady gaze. "What's that?"

"I read this somewhere, okay? Or heard it at a movie. It's a quote."

"Okay."

"It's better to have loved and lost than never to have loved at all."

"Love?" Sandra almost shrieked. "There's nothing, absolutely nothing, even vaguely resembling love between McCloud and me."

Letty flashed a knowing grin. "You slept with him."

"Slept with him? I..." Her outrage sluiced away from her. "I did. And I'm not real proud of that."

"Why not? Did he throw you out of bed and tell you never to come back?"

"No, of course not." Sandra patted the water from her face with a plush white towel. "He asked me to stay. Then he set up this elaborate con job to get me back down here."

"And you've got a problem with that?" Letty shook her head slowly from side to side. "Jeez, Sandra, I thought I was dumb about men, but you're worse than me."

"I resent his playing all these sneaky little games." Sandra stared into the mirror, trying to be honest with herself and with Letty. "It's all wrong. Even if he wasn't a con man, I couldn't possibly have any sort of relationship with him."

"Why not?"

"Well, for one thing, I'm an attorney in a big city and I love my career." At least, she used to love her career, before she discovered that being a partner meant being a slave to the whims of the firm. "McCloud is a buffalo rancher. There is absolutely no way our life-styles could match up."

"I kind of understand." Letty squinted her big blue eyes to concentrate. She was a good person, but not a real heavy thinker. "Here's a good way to figure out if a guy is good for you or not. Imagine you're up in a plane. A Cessna. At twenty thousand feet. There's a malfunction. We're going down. We're down to nineteen thousand. Eighteen thousand. And there's only one parachute. I ask myself if he's going to give it to me? Or keep it for himself?"

"Pretty dramatic test. What would your ex do?"

"Heck, he'd probably push me out of the plane to soften his landing. The guy's not right for a relationship."

"Agreed," Sandra said.

"But it's been almost a year now, and I still haven't found anybody who turns me on like he used to do."

She sighed. "Don't throw this McCloud away too fast, Sandra. You know what they say—Good men are hard to find." She chuckled. "You know, that Pablo is kind of cute."

WHEN THE TWO WOMEN joined McCloud in his office, he noticed an additional degree of hostility in Sandra's manner. He hadn't thought it possible, but her jaw was even more outthrust, and her eyes were as cold as a snowy day on Raton Pass. She was a woman who was determined to pick a fight, and McCloud wasn't in the mood to be goaded. If she wanted to square off and do battle, she'd better be prepared for a thrashing.

He stood behind his desk. "Well, Sandra, decided to believe in my quest, have you?"

"I have not."

"But you're here, and so anxious to start hunting that you want to review the maps."

Her fists stuck on her hips. "I wouldn't walk one mile, not even one yard, not even one inch, to look for your mythical city of gold. As far as I'm concerned, the only Eldorado I believe in is a car manufactured by Cadillac."

Letty stepped between them. "How about those maps, McCloud? Can we take a look at the search area?"

He gestured to a ten-foot-long oak table at the back of his office. Paper covered most of the surface. "Help yourself, ladies."

"I got a question for you." Letty planted herself in front of his desk. "Suppose you were on an airplane that was going down and Sandra was with you.

There's only one parachute. What're you going to do?''

Sandra tugged at her friend's arm. "I don't think we really need to—"

"There's no way of fixing the plane?" McCloud interrupted.

"Please forget that question," Sandra advised. "Come on, Letty, let's take a look at the maps."

"Hold on, Sandra. I want to hear what he says."

McCloud said, "There's only one chute, right?"

"You got it."

"And we definitely have to ditch the plane?"

"That's right."

"Here's what I'd do. I'd put on the parachute." He circled the desk swiftly, grasped Sandra's arm and pulled her close to him, crushing her against his chest. "I'd hold Sandra like this and we'd jump together. We'd both survive."

"Wow!" Letty applauded. "That's really smart."

He released Sandra with a gallant smile. "Sorry if I mussed you. I was just making a point."

Her blood hammered in her temples. "Don't you ever do that again!"

"Save your life in an airplane crash? But, Sandra, I wouldn't ever let you fall."

"If you touch me again, I'll—"

"What? Sue me?"

He turned his back and went to the table where he spread a map that was three feet by four.

Sandra inhaled deeply, mentally blessing the courtroom experience that had taught her to stay calm under adversarial pressure. Because her encounters with McCloud were definitely placing him in the position of being an enemy.

Her lips drew into a straight thin line, and she noticed that Letty had stepped back to avoid the explosion. Letty, of course, was familiar with Sandra in this mood. Letty had seen her in action in a courtroom where Sandra had chomped grown men into tiny bite-size pieces and spit them out.

"All right, McCloud." Sandra stood opposite him at the table. "Let's see your treasure map."

"I don't have anything that says X marks the spot. If I did, I wouldn't have been searching for eight years. This map is an overview."

It was a detailed topographical representation of the area. About half of the map had been marked off with small black squares.

"The crossed-off part shows places I've already covered on foot."

"What's the scale on this?" Letty asked.

"Half an inch equals a mile. This area is about one hundred miles by seventy miles. But it's not really that much. The search only pertains to canyon lands and plateaus."

"Why?"

"Because," Sandra explained, "this quest is based on a folk yarn. In that highly improbable story, the land is described as having high walls that touch the sky. Is that correct, McCloud?"

"Correct."

"And berries," Sandra continued. "I seem to recall something about an abundance of berries. Have you done a berry survey of the land?"

He regarded her coldly, and she took his disdain as a compliment. She was getting to him, chipping away at his quest and exposing it for the sham that it was. "Well, McCloud? What about the berries?"

"In seven hundred years, the local flora has probably changed. However, the mention of berries—which remains consistent in several versions of this legend—is one reason I believe the search in this area is justified. Higher elevations and desert have very little vegetation."

"Of course, if we stick to the legend," Sandra said sarcastically, "I should be able to whip out the door and march right directly to this city of gold."

"I don't get it," Letty interrupted. "Why are you supposed to be able to find it?"

"Because I am the reincarnation of Dawn Fire." She spun and met his glare with her own anger. "Isn't that right, McCloud? Isn't that what we're doing here, reliving the legend? I'm supposed to warn the warriors, and then the one brave who believes in me will come to my hogan in the night and . . ."

Her words faded as she remembered the story he'd told her at the campfire. There was one warrior who loved Dawn Fire. He'd made love to her. Just as McCloud had done with her. The following day, Dawn Fire had departed. Just as Sandra had done. The similarity between actual events and legend was annoyingly coincidental. And a little scary, too. What if there was some basis to this weird, mythical story?

"What else?" Letty asked. "What else happens in the legend?"

"Ask McCloud. He believes in it." Suddenly Sandra was confused. She wanted to be near him, but she couldn't stand to be in the same room with him. Grabbing a handful of maps, she pivoted and went to the door. "I'll be in my room."

Her retreat was quick, but deliberate. She didn't want to give the impression of running away. Her natural urge was to fight McCloud, but she wasn't sure what or why she was fighting. He hadn't been deliberately cruel or unfair to her. Though his quest might end up costing her parents a small fortune, it was their money after all. If Emma and Thornton wanted to throw their windfall away on a packet of magic beans, it wasn't up to Sandra to rescue them.

She'd barely had time to flop down on the bed, realizing that the mattress was too soft and the comforter billowed around her, when she heard the unmistakable thunk of his boot heels on the hardwood floor.

McCloud yanked open the door.

She snapped, "Don't you believe in knocking?"

"I want some answers."

"Fine. But you'll have to come up with intelligent questions." She tried to prop herself up on the bed, but it really was terribly soft. She was wallowing in bedcovers. "Because I've had more than enough fooling around. Get to it, McCloud. Then leave me alone."

He strode to the window and pulled aside the curtain to look outside. Beyond the barn, a sprawling mountain panorama faded into near foothills and plateaus. Even closer were fields, mingling green stretches of irrigated land with untended patches of brown. The land, he thought, was uncomplicated. With care, the soil blossomed. With neglect, it lay fallow. The buffalo fed and grew. Simple. The natural scheme of things was simple. Why were his dealings with Sandra so complicated?

He glanced back at her as she struggled to be dignified while drowning in bedspreads. She looked so damn cute, he wanted to pick her up in his arms and cuddle her. But her angry response to his little hug earlier made him reconsider. It might be safer to cozy up to a rattlesnake.

Keeping his voice noncommittal, he said, "You're angry. Why?"

"You don't want to know, McCloud."

"Hell, yes. I sure do. If we're going to be together for the next two weeks, let's get this squared right now. I don't want to waste time trying to guess why you're angry. Or what I've done to offend you."

"You want plain talk?"

"That's right."

"Well, McCloud, here's the bottom line." She looked away from him as she spoke. "I don't trust you."

Chapter Six

McCloud could stand being called stubborn or lazy or crazy. At times, he was all those things. But untrustworthy? That was the worst thing, bar none, that she could have said. He was an honest man. Always. And if she couldn't see that, if she didn't understand that essential core inside him, then the hell with her. He dropped the curtain at her bedroom window and headed for the door.

"McCloud," she called after him, "don't you want to know why I don't trust you?"

"No." He took another step away from her.

"Don't want to hear it, huh? Afraid to face the truth?"

Now she was accusing him of being a coward! His jaw was so tense that he could only manage one syllable. "Why?"

"Your investment scheme with my parents is risky."

He turned and glared. "What do you mean?"

"At the very least, they lose two years' interest on their money. At worst, you could lose it all."

"Not possible." Why couldn't she see that? Why was she so determined to make him a bad guy? "It's clear-cut. I put the money into escrow and, after two years, I pay it back.''

''That's not how your contract is worded. The terms are vague. You have complete control of the monies. There's no protection for them. And you should have advised them to talk to me first.'' He heard the bed-springs creaking as she shifted her position. ''But you didn't. You came to Denver yourself, to meet me and charm me off my feet. And you were hoping I wouldn't look into the contract. Correct?''

He could have protested, could have informed her that he wasn't a cheap rip-off artist. Hell, he didn't need to be. His buffalo ranch was profitable.

''And that's not all,'' she continued. ''You got me back here using your Navajo contacts at my law firm. I was coerced, against my will, to come here because of your lousy folk legend. How can I possibly trust a man who pulls that kind of stuff?''

It wouldn't do a damn bit of good to tell this un-reasonable woman that he had nothing to do with Martin White Horse's demands. He pivoted and glared at her.

''And when you made love to me...'' Her voice cracked slightly. She was on her knees in the middle of the too-soft bed, almost bouncing amid the quilts.

Finally, McCloud thought, she was getting to the truth. This was the real reason she was angry. Her passionate arguments about contracts and the law firm were a smoke screen for this greater womanly passion.

In an unsteady voice, she said, ''I might have over-looked the alleged 'chance' meeting in Denver. I might have been convinced to work with you on the contract. And maybe, if I dredged up every ounce of understanding in my soul, I could have accepted Martin White Horse and his legend. But when we made love, McCloud, you betrayed me in a way that I can never forgive.'' Sandra inhaled a deep breath, obviously fighting for control. ''You made love to me because you wanted me to look the other way on the contract.''

''That's a pretty cold accusation.'' What kind of coyote did she think he was? ''You don't believe that, do you?''

''Yes! No!'' Her hands flew up to cover her ears. ''I don't want to hear any more lies.''

''How the hell can I be lying? You won't let me say anything.''

''That's right. I won't.'' She leapt to her feet in the middle of the bed. ''You've lied. You've manipulated. And you've schemed. I can't trust you.''

''Are you done?''

''Yes.'' Her small chin jutted as she threw down the challenge. ''You said you wanted to clear the air. Here's your chance to prove you have even one sincere bone in your body.''

''You might not want to hear what I have to say. Are you sure you want me to speak my mind?''

''Go ahead.'' In the back of her mind, Sandra cringed. But she braced herself. Might as well get this over with. He couldn't hurt her much more than he already had. ''I'm ready.''

He crossed the room and stood beside the bed. ''I made love to you because I wanted you. You, Sandra Carberry. You got inside my head. When I carried you back inside that poor excuse for a tent, there was no other woman in the universe except for you. It might have been destiny because I've never felt exactly like that before. Like you were part of me. As if, without you, I would be incomplete. I had to have you.''

She blinked. This wasn't what she expected.

In a low voice, he continued, ''The way I feel about you has nothing to do with money or investments. And it sure as hell doesn't have any weird connection to the legend. I don't believe you're Dawn Fire or a *bruja* or anyone other than an obstinate lady lawyer from Denver who is making me crazy.''

''I can leave,'' she said. ''If I make you so crazy, I can leave at any time.''

''But you can't.'' A slow smile curved his lips. His voice was a low sexy growl. ''You're stuck here with me. Like you said before, Sandra, it's your job.''

She opened her mouth to object, then closed it again. He was right. Mr. Jessop had made it clear that she had a duty to the firm. If she left, she'd be taking a backward step in her career. On the other hand, no one could force her to stay here. Not if the situation really was intolerable.

''You'll be fired if you leave,'' McCloud said.

''Not really. Not unless Mr. Jessop wants the world's biggest sexual harassment suit slapped against him.''

''You don't want to go.'' The intensity of his gaze mesmerized her, seduced logic, reduced her anger to a whisper of discontent. ''You want to stay here. With me.''

''This isn't about you,'' she protested.

''Don't lie to me, Sandra.''

Standing there on the bed, she felt suddenly outmatched. Her emotions had driven her to behave in a silly manner, and he was acting like a full-grown, adult man. Intelligent and wise and so sexy that—if she'd been able to be completely honest with herself—she would have been in his arms instead of in his face.

She drew herself up as best she could and said, "I'll stay because I promised that I would. And I don't go back on my word."

He nodded, returned to the door and opened it.

"Hey, McCloud."

"Yes, Sandra?"

"If there is a city of gold, I'll find it. You can count on that."

He smiled and left the room, closing the door behind him.

Sandra crumpled. All the air went out of her body, and she sank down in a boneless heap on the ultrasoft bed. She pulled a pillow over her face, smothering an urge to scream or to weep. But she didn't cave in to either impulse. Control, she needed control. But nothing made sense anymore. She wanted to grab McCloud and shake him. She wanted to grab McCloud and make love to him with all of the raging passion in her soul.

"But I am a Professional," she reminded herself. "With a capital *P*, and I can handle this job like any other job."

She'd prove to McCloud that her job wasn't an excuse to stay here. She'd show him that the only reason she'd come here was to search for El Dorado. And, when she'd proved that his city of gold was nothing more than an empty folk tale, she'd demand her parents' money back. Then she would leave with her personal dignity intact.

At least, that was what she intended to do.

Pulling herself together, she snatched up the small map she'd taken with her and strode down the hall. In the office, she found Letty sitting at the large table, pouring over a series of maps. She glanced up, slightly distracted. "Sandra? You okay?"

"I'm fine."

"Good, then come over here."

Letty spread one of the maps on the table. Her manner was brisk and businesslike. Though this robust blonde in a pink jumpsuit might not be brilliant when it came to human relationships, she was a highly skilled pilot, qualified on small planes and minijets as well as helicopters.

"What is it?" Sandra asked.

"I thought you said that McCloud hadn't done surveying on these sites, that he was just riding through the hills."

Sandra nodded.

"These maps are showing me a totally different picture."

"What are they?"

"Aerial photos. And they weren't made by an amateur. He's got these canyons plotted perfectly."

Sandra leaned over the huge photograph. It showed topography without depth. To Sandra's untrained eye, the picture had some interesting artistic features, but she couldn't make sense of the overhead view. It took a while for Letty to accustom Sandra to the photo as she pointed out a winding river and the shadows that outlined mesquite and shrubs and trees.

"Everything is foreshortened," Letty explained. "Imagine someone taking a picture of the top of your head. You wouldn't have a body, just a shadow of a body."

"Fascinating," Sandra said.

"The master is taken with a series of exposures. It's really a composite of several photos. A plane flies overhead and an aerial photographer aims a camera that almost works like a movie camera. Then the photos are blended into one seamless picture to show all the plateaus and canyons between from the same angle." She pulled out a smaller picture. "Here's a close-up of one canyon wall."

At first glance, the canyon looked like blobs of shadow and light, messy silhouettes. Letty pointed to one space, wider than the others. "Right here. This is some kind of a cave beneath an overhang. Ever been to Mesa Verde?"

"Sure, the cliff dwellings that could be Anasazi ruins." A small excitement built inside Sandra. Could it be possible that they'd already located the city of gold? "Letty, would Mesa Verde look like this from the air?"

"It might."

"But it didn't," McCloud's voice said from behind them.

Both women were startled as he returned to the office on silent moccasined feet. He'd changed his clothes, and his ebony black hair was still wet from the shower.

"On the back of that photo," he said, "there's a note and a date. There was nothing in that canyon, except for a big vacant cave."

"This is pretty fancy photography," Letty said. "Must have cost you a bundle."

"Wasn't cheap, but I got a good deal with a pilot and an aerial photographer who traded me their time for buffalo meat."

While he and Letty talked about photogrammetry and measurements and laser-sensitive equipment, Sandra flipped through the stacks and stacks of maps and photos. Not only was their discussion so far removed from her area of expertise that she felt handicapped by her own ignorance, she also didn't want to be too close to McCloud. His presence was too disturbing. The clean scent of his body, fresh from the shower, fired up all kinds of inappropriate desires within her. And she was determined not to give him the satisfaction of knowing how much he aroused her.

She was here to do a job, to find El Dorado. And, frankly, these maps had given her a new respect for his methods. Though Martin White Horse had mentioned McCloud's use of technology, she had no idea that he'd employed such detailed methods to further his quest. Instead, she'd pictured him setting out, like Don Quixote, on his trusty steed, Rosinante, to poke his way through the windmills.

The pictures in her hands began to have some kind of form and pattern. She returned to one of the main overhead views and turned it upside down. Then sideways. Her artistic sense, inherited from her mother, came into play as she studied the natural design inherent in the topography of these lands. She saw the flow of rivers, the details of local vegetation. Some areas were verdant with undulating hillsides, others were flat desert with sharply defined ridges and crevasses.

The vast scope of his search impressed her, and she realized that this was more than a weekend hobby. McCloud was dead serious about finding this city of gold. He wasn't a total crackpot.

"What do you think?" Letty asked her.

Sandra blinked and looked up. "About what?"

"McCloud says he's done fly-bys in a bunch of these canyons. And the most he's ever found is a reason to look harder in some places. So, what do you think, Sandra? Is it worth it for me to stick around?"

McCloud also waited for her answer. His cooperative attitude gave every appearance of innocence, but she knew better. He was arrogance personified. He knew the depth of his technological research had surprised her, and he couldn't wait for her to admit it. Gritting her teeth, Sandra asked, "What do you think, McCloud? Would a helicopter search be of value?"

"It could save some time," he conceded. "I've narrowed the search area considerably since the last time I was up in a plane."

"And that was a plane," Letty said. "Not a chopper. You'll see more this way."

"Couple of problems," he explained. "The city was designed to be invisible unless you were right upon it, so a straight overhead view is almost worthless."

Sandra pointed to the map. "Is that why you only have a few of these large scanning shots?"

"Right. Basically, those pictures were for a photogrammetry specialist who put together the big map which I use to mark off areas where I've already searched."

She swallowed her impulse to snap at him, to express her heartfelt belief that the city of gold was fantasy and he was nothing more than the world's sexiest con man. "What other kind of research have you done?"

He pulled open a file drawer on a large oak cabinet. It was neatly sorted with manila folders. "Archaeological and anthropological data. These are transcripts of the various Native American legends from the Hopi, Navajo, Ute and Apache. In the rear section is research on Coronado and his search for El Dorado."

When she joined him at the cabinet, standing with the neatly cataloged folders between them, he abruptly closed the file and yanked open a lower drawer. "In here is all the legal work—the deeds and lease agreements. I suppose you'll be more interested in that."

"You suppose wrong," she cooly responded. "I am here as a representative of Jessop, Feldner and White. My purpose is to find the object of this quest, not to research the legality of your investment scheme."

Sandra shoved the lower drawer shut with her foot. For a moment, there was no obstacle between them. Only thin air separated her body from his, and Sandra had a thoroughly insane desire to bridge that space. It would be so simple to take one small step forward into his arms.

Very quickly, she put a barrier between them, opening the archaeology/anthropology drawer and busily reading the labels at the top of the folders.

McCloud returned to the map table. "Okay, Letty, how much area can we cover tomorrow?"

"Depends. There's weather to consider. And I'm not sure how much time it'll take to cover any particular spot. Let's map out a promising sector and we'll see how it goes."

Half listening to their conversation, Sandra absently pulled a fat manila folder that was marked Legend. Inside were several versions of the story he'd told her. Each was marked with a name, a date and a tribe. They appeared to be arranged alphabetically by the name of the storyteller. She flipped to the rear and looked for Thomas Sweetwater, the man who had told McCloud the legend ten years ago.

She glanced down the page. The story was slightly expanded but essentially the same as the one he'd told her. Behind the Sweetwater version of the legend, she found a verbatim transcript in halting English from a Hopi woman who claimed to be a descendant of the woman she called Star Fire. Wasn't it Dawn Fire?

While McCloud and Letty discussed fuel stops and the quickest way from one point to the next, Sandra skimmed several other pages. Though the legend remained fairly consistent, the woman's name varied. Star Fire. White Moon. Dawn Fire. Not of Dark. White Dawn. Sun Lady.

"Always something celestial," she murmured.

When Elena summoned them for dinner, Sandra tucked a couple of files under her arm and dropped them off in her bedroom on the way to the huge dining room table. There might be a clue there. Somewhere in all these pieces, a solution might be found. *If* the city existed, she reminded herself.

At the long dinner table, Pablo had seated himself next to Letty and McCloud sat at the head. Though Sandra would have preferred to be as far away from McCloud as possible, he was holding out the chair to his right for her. She couldn't take another seat without being out-and-out rude. It was the only other place Elena had set.

Steeling herself, Sandra slipped into her seat. "Thank you."

His hand brushed her shoulder as he held her chair, and his touch felt like fire, branding her skin. She spent most of the meal avoiding eye contact with him. That was the most devastating, she thought—looking into his turquoise eyes and remembering the night they'd been together.

Instead, she concentrated on the barely perceptible mating dance of Pablo and Letty. He kept stealing surreptitious looks at this big blond woman pilot. Only after Elena served dessert did Pablo turn to McCloud to mention a business concern. "While you are gone, I might need to hire a new man."

"Why?"

"Rustlers. We need to spend more time riding herd."

"Rustling buffalo?" Sandra asked.

"They steal anything," Pablo informed her. "Cattle, buffalo. Even sheep."

Letty chuckled. "This sounds like something out of the Old West."

"I guess people haven't changed much since the old days," Sandra said. "As long as there's something worth stealing, there's somebody there to steal it."

Pablo nodded. "It is true."

Sandra looked briefly at McCloud. "Are these same guys, the same *hombres,* who you thought might follow you and take their spoils from the city of gold?"

"Possibly."

"And why are they at large? What's wrong with your sheriff's department?"

"The sheriff is not at fault," Pablo said defensively. "And I would say that even if he was not my cousin. Every time he arrests one, they get their bail, they get parole, they get off. *Adiós.*"

Sandra was extremely familiar with this complaint. "Then the problem is the legal system."

"Yes." Pablo frowned. "My cousin and his family are in danger from these *hombres*. The system is not good."

McCloud added, "There's only one prosecuting district attorney for his whole area, and he spends most of his time in the towns and cities. Frankly, our local sheriff would have a better chance if he was allowed to shoot first and ask questions later."

Pablo pushed away from the table. "McCloud? Can I hire a man?"

"Go ahead. Do it tomorrow if you think it's necessary."

Pablo turned to Letty and grinned widely. "Before it is dark, will you show me your helicopter?"

"Sure. If you'll show me the horses."

Sandra noticed that Pablo placed his hand at the small of Letty's back to guide her through the door to the kitchen, and Letty didn't object. As they passed from earshot, Sandra heard her friend say, "Let me ask you something, Pablo. If you and me were up in an airplane and it was going down, and there was only one chute..."

Sandra shook her head and laughed. Letty and Pablo? To say the least, they would make an interesting couple. A clear case of opposites attracting.

Not unlike McCloud and herself.

But, of course, it wasn't the same. Letty and Pablo had no reason for antagonism. She sipped her coffee and mused. "Do you think they'll hit it off? Letty and Pablo?"

"He'll probably win her over. I don't know how he does it, but Pablo has a string of ladies three miles long."

"I'm sorry to hear that," Sandra said. Swift seductions were probably the local habit. McCloud hadn't wasted much time in getting her into bed. "Do most of the men from around here have a string of ladies three miles long?"

"Are you asking about me, Sandra?"

"Certainly not," she protested. "Why would I care about you?"

"No reason." He scooted back his chair. "Let's take our coffee on the porch and watch the sun go down."

"I think not." Her instincts told her to get as far away from him as possible. "I'm awfully tired, and—"

"Scared?" he challenged.

Terrified, she thought. Being close to him was hazardous to her mental health, but she sure wasn't going to let him know how much he upset her equilibrium. "You don't scare me, McCloud."

"Good, then let's go onto the porch."

The wide porch stretched all the way across the front of the house. Long, low benches spanned the area beneath the windows, and there were a couple of rocking chairs, but McCloud sat on the stoop. With his coffee cup cradled in his hands, he gazed toward the western skies and sighed.

The sunset was magnificent, with burnished golds and reds and pinks painted on a celestial canvas as the sun dipped lower behind the San Juans. The grandeur extended across the foothills and mesquite-covered plains. Even the clumps of cottonwood trees seemed touched by springtime magic, their leaves gilded with the last light of day.

On an average day in Denver, Sandra considered the setting sun to be an annoyance as the last glistening rays got in her eyes and bothered her on her drive from office to home. Most often, she missed it altogether. After-work hours were her time for working out at the Athletic Club, swimming in a chlorinated pool, drying in sumptuous surroundings and rushing home where she kept busy with the paperwork she hadn't completed in the office. Or she'd dash off to fulfill a social obligation.

McCloud patted the stoop beside him. "Sit down, Sandra."

So close to him? Nearness was dangerous to her self-control, but she could handle it. She'd have to learn to handle it. On this quest, they would be together frequently. Constantly.

She sat. Her posture mimicked his as she leaned forward and rested her elbows on her knees. She held her coffee cup, inhaled the rich fragrance. Her belly was comfortably full from dinner. Her gaze fixed on the changing patterns of brilliant color in the skies.

And then the sun was gone. The colors in the sky began to fade like a delicate wash across one of her mother's watercolor paintings. "Have my parents been here?" she asked.

"Yes. They came for an afternoon and spent almost a week. I enjoyed having them. Wonderful people. Both of them are deep thinkers, but they haven't lost the capacity to be thrilled to death over a clump of daisies... or a sunset."

"Wonderful?" She chuckled. "I didn't often hear them described that way while I was growing up."

"No?"

"They've never had a terrific concept of time. My mother constantly missed appointments with my teachers. And when it came to paying the bills, neither of them managed to remember when it was the first of the month." She remembered as if it were yesterday. "The collection companies didn't think Emma and Thornton were so wonderful. I started fielding those calls when I was about fourteen."

"They didn't ask you to do that, did they?"

"No, of course not." Tossing her head, she tried to shake away the unpleasant memories. "They never demanded that I take on the task of balancing the budgets and coming up with excuses for the bill collectors. But somebody had to do it. Somebody had to be responsible."

"And that somebody was you."

She hunched to ease the sudden tension between her shoulders. "I can't complain. Growing up fast was a good preparation for the rest of my life. Responsibilities don't frighten me, and I don't expect anyone to take care of me."

"You've done well for yourself," he said, "making partner in a law firm."

"And that," she said, "is a whole other set of problems."

"How so?"

She hesitated. Sandra wasn't accustomed to sharing her inner thoughts, her doubts and difficulties. The face she showed to the world was utterly cool, and she didn't like for her weaknesses to be exposed. "You wouldn't understand," she finally said.

"About responsibilities? Hell, yes I would. This might look like an idyllic ranch to you, but it's a business. There's a regular full-time staff of four people at the ranch and ten in the field, and sometimes I've hired up to forty—"

"Really?" she interrupted. "Where are they?"

"Out with the herd. They're cowboys, Sandra. I've got over fifteen hundred head, not including the newborn spring calves."

She tried to imagine that many buffalo. The thought was overwhelming. "Where are they?"

"On the range. I want the buffalo to run free, to reclaim this land where once they dominated." He shrugged. "Maybe it's the Indian blood in me."

"Are you part Navajo?"

"Ute," he replied. "My mother was half Ute. But I never lived on the reservation. My Ute grandmother passed away before I was ten years old."

"Was she the first to tell you the El Dorado legends?"

"I don't remember her stories very well. I remember once picking yellow flowers with her. And each time we took a flower, we thanked Mother Earth for her beauty and bounty."

"Was that out here, on the buffalo ranch?"

"No, we lived in Alamosa when I was little. My father owned a hardware store there and my mother was an English professor at the college, Adams State. I was twelve when my father bought the land out here and we started the ranch. I've been running this place by myself for the past seven years. So, I know a thing or two about being responsible."

"And you enjoy it?"

He shrugged. "Most of the time I love it."

"Then why aren't you content with just this?" Sandra felt herself being drawn toward him as she discovered this new side to his character. "Why go off on wild searches?"

"A man needs a dream. Isn't that why you went into law?"

"Yes," she said firmly. "I wanted to make a difference."

"And why do you look so sad when you talk about your career?"

"I don't. I'm not." She wasn't about to share her doubts and confusions with him. How could she? She didn't even trust him. Sandra pinched her lips together, and they sat in silence.

Her coffee cup was empty, and the night had snuggled around them. The moment reminded her of another nightfall, when they'd sat at a campfire, and her heart had been set on fire. The embers were still there, but Sandra maintained a careful control of the small flame. She couldn't allow the sparks to become a wanton brushfire that might consume and destroy her.

"Sandra?"

His baritone reverberated through her. She could feel her passions rising. "Yes?"

"What do you want from life? What's your dream?"

To hold him. To kiss him. To make love to him, again. She shifted uncomfortably on the hard porch. He'd posed a question she could not, would not, answer. And yet, when she glanced toward him, his knowing gaze seemed to read her mind. His encouraging smile urged her to tell him how very much she wanted him.

"Sandra," he whispered. His voice caressed her. "I think I know what you want."

"Sleep." Quickly she stood and yawned. "I'm dreaming of sleep. I'd best be getting to bed now. We'll have a busy day tomorrow."

He stood beside her, and she could feel the warmth of his body reaching for her, drawing her closer.

"Good night, McCloud."

She fled into the ranch house, stumbling down the hall to her bedroom where she collapsed onto her too-soft bed. Her heart was beating a mile a minute. Her arms wanted to hold him; her lips yearned for his kiss. There was a sensual tingling that chased through her veins and gathered in the most private part of her anatomy.

Irresponsible! Impulsive! Insane! She didn't want to feel like this, but it was becoming horribly obvious that she wouldn't be able to ignore her passions much longer.

Chapter Seven

The next morning, Sandra wished she hadn't so enthusiastically devoured every spicy morsel of Elena's *huevos rancheros* breakfast. The eggs and salsa congealed in a queasy lump in her stomach as she took her place in the rear of the helicopter. Even worse, McCloud climbed in beside her and sat close enough that their thighs brushed. She recoiled as if bitten by a rattler. His mere presence had an unsettling effect upon her.

She avoided looking at him and tapped Letty on the shoulder. "Should I sit up front with you?"

But Pablo had taken that seat, and Letty seemed pleased by his unwavering attention.

"You can see from back there," Letty told her. "I want all of you to strap yourselves in. It's a clear day, but wind currents are always tricky in canyons. Could be a bumpy ride."

Sandra groaned as the rotor blades picked up speed and the copter lifted off. Under normal circumstances, Sandra wasn't a nervous flier, but she hadn't slept well on the overly soft bed that wrapped around her like a cloying embrace. She was stiff. Every fiber of her body complained, but none so loudly as the helicopter's roar that permeated the soundproof earphones she wore. The earphones were equipped with an intercom so they could all speak to each other easily. A slight, steady vibration accompanied the ride. Sandra turned away from McCloud, closed her eyes and tried to relax.

Last night, when she had almost given up on the probability of getting any real rest, she sorted through the Legend file, discovering that McCloud's initial telling was pretty much the standard story, including the unexplained deaths of children, the warriors preparing for battle and Dawn Fire's leading the way to a golden city. Consistent landmarks seemed to be high walls, suggesting a canyon, and an abundance of berries and good soil, which made Sandra think that there must be rivers or a spring nearby.

Several stories spoke of the summer sun and, though the descriptions of Dawn Fire varied, they always contained something that referred to a sunrise or a sunset or the sun itself or the moon and stars. There seemed to be a theme emphasizing life-giving heat. Dawn Fire almost always played the role of an earth goddess, encouraging the people to plant and harvest rather than to make war.

And the warrior who made love to her was always mentioned. Though Sandra could assume that the anthropological theme was fertility—hence, the conception of seven sons—she couldn't help making a more personal interpretation. Her image of the warrior brave was McCloud. A strong man. A man who dared to defy the other braves in his tribe. A man who could become obsessed with a woman. Was that possible of McCloud? He'd given hints that he could care deeply for her, even love her. But was that another con job?

At breakfast, she'd tried to discern if he truly cared for her. Of course she couldn't come right out and ask if he would follow her to the ends of the earth. But there must be some way of testing, some clever method of cross-examination.

Unfortunately, McCloud had been preoccupied at the breakfast table. There were business matters that he and Pablo had to discuss. Also, as soon as Elena learned they would be making a stop in Alamosa to refuel, she'd come up with a grocery list. Usually, Sandra would approve of such responsible behavior, but today...now...with McCloud...she wanted a wildly obsessed lover.

The helicopter took a little bounce, and Sandra opened her eyes. She'd always thought of helicopter travel as being slow, but yesterday she'd learned that when Letty wanted to make time, the landscape passed below them in a dizzying blur. This helicopter was designed for sight-seeing, and the bubble window gave a clear, almost three-hundred-and-sixty-degree view.

Over the headset, she listened to Letty informing Pablo on the simplicity of handling one of these flying machines. When he asked if he might take the controls, Sandra and McCloud replied in unison. "No!"

"For your support," Pablo said wryly, "I thank you."

"Nothing personal," McCloud said. "But this isn't like riding a bicycle where if you fall off you get a bump on your butt. A mistake can have some real bad consequences."

"Not to mention that this is one expensive bird," Letty added. "Sorry, Pablo, honey. I just can't let you."

"Okay, Letty. You're the boss."

He patted her on the shoulder, and the good-natured gesture lingered a few seconds too long. Sandra noticed that Letty didn't object. Apparently, Pablo had passed her one-parachute test for suitable relationship material.

How simple, Sandra thought. Letty was able to fall right into a relationship without any of the angst that Sandra went through. Why? Why did she have to make everything so doggone complicated for herself? She should have been content to accept her night with McCloud as a one-night fling—terribly imprudent and nothing to be proud of—but a single mistake. Instead, she was in the back of a helicopter, searching for a probably nonexistent city of gold and forced to be in the presence of a man who made her blood boil.

It wasn't fair. Right now, when her career was going so well and everything in her life should have been rosy, she felt blue. Sandra pulled up her chin. *Get a grip! Stop feeling sorry for yourself!* As her mother the artist would have reminded her, mixing rose and blue gave purple, the color of royalty and strength.

Her gaze drifted over toward McCloud, whose focus was concentrated on the maps that he'd spread across his knees. He was wearing wire-frame reading glasses that made him look studious, serious and... sexy.

He peeked over the frames, caught her gaze and smiled. It was just a hint of friendly camaraderie, but Sandra felt a warm blush rising in her cheeks. What was it about him, anyway? From every angle, in every mood, he provoked a sensuous reaction in her.

"Thoroughly inappropriate," she muttered.

"What?" came the echo of three voices.

Sandra's words had, of course, been picked up on the headset. "Nothing," she said quickly.

"Are we headed the right way?" Letty looked over her shoulder.

"Follow this creek," McCloud instructed. "We've got about five miles to go before we get to the first area I wanted to cover."

The landscape was far enough below them to look like an illustrated relief map. On either side of the river, there were trees and greenery, then the desert and mesquite spread in a monotonous beige. The mountains that nearly encircled them were distant and blue with higher peaks etched in glacial snowcaps. Clouds and sky surrounded them.

McCloud directed Letty into the first canyon and they slowed to a hover speed.

The lump in Sandra's stomach twisted in a wretched knot. A disgusting, metallic taste tingled in her mouth, and she thought she might throw up. She pressed her lips together to keep from gagging.

"Sandra?" McCloud touched her shoulder. "Are you all right?"

She nodded, not trusting herself to speak, and forced herself to stare blindly at the cliffside.

Letty hovered about twenty feet above the canyon floor, and the whirring action of the rotor blades kicked up a fury of dust and loose branches directly beneath them.

"Higher?" Letty questioned. "Lower?"

"Not lower." McCloud craned his neck to see the ground below. "We're disturbing the land."

"Only a couple of rattlesnakes and bunny rabbits," Pablo said. "No big deal, boss."

"But it is," he contradicted. "We are seeking something from the earth. What can we hope to find if we disturb the land?"

Pablo muttered a good-natured curse, then turned to look at Sandra. "This is his Indian blood talking."

"And this is an old argument between us," McCloud explained. "Pablo is a practical man. He comes from a family of farmers and ranchers."

"I'm proud of my family."

"As you should be," Letty said supportively.

"This isn't about family," McCloud said. "It's about the earth. The sacredness and the limitations of the earth."

"What limits?" There was a hint of exasperation in Pablo's voice. With a sweeping gesture, he indicated that vast untouched acreage that surrounded them. "There will always be more land."

"No, my friend. There is no guarantee of endless bounty. There may come a day when the rivers run dry. When we take, we must replenish." To Letty, he said, "Go higher, so we're not disturbing the snakes and rabbits."

Sandra's stomach had settled enough to ask, "If we go higher, will we be able to thoroughly search in this canyon?"

"Pretty much," he said. "If we're looking for a city built into the cliffside, like Mesa Verde, we might get a hint of an overhang. Then we can descend and check it out. On the other hand, if the city of gold is built low to the earth and has been reduced to mostly rubble, we won't see it.''

"Not at all?"

"It's not likely. My research indicates that the city was built six or seven hundred years ago. It could be almost completely obliterated and the only indication might be an odd rock formation. That's why I've been combing these canyons on foot.''

Again, Sandra realized how little she knew about this quest. In her mind's eye, she'd pictured a real city with towers and buildings and doors and windows. Of course, it was far more likely that McCloud was looking for an archaeologist's vision of a city, requiring excavation and deep searching. When considered from his viewpoint, the idea of a helicopter search seemed shallow and probably fruitless. She sighed. "So much for finding this place in a couple of hours, eh?''

"The odds are against it." His turquoise eyes sparkled. "But you are a very lucky woman. I'd go along with almost any suggestion you made.''

Any suggestion? She wondered what he would say if she suggested abandoning the search, spending the next two weeks in bed searching for new horizons in purely physical pleasure. A quick glance at McCloud, his warm gaze and the subtle grin that appeared beneath his high cheekbones, gave her an answer. That was a quest he'd be happy to indulge in . . . if she were insane enough to suggest it.

"Not likely," she muttered into the headset.

"What?" they chorused.

"Nothing."

They whisked down two more canyons, finding nothing of note. On the next pass, down an extremely long and narrow stretch, Letty pointed. "Look over there."

A young man had stepped into the sunlight. He was shirtless, as if he'd been awakened by the helicopter's whirring intrusion.

"What do you think he's doing out here?" Letty asked.

"Pull up," Pablo commanded.

"Why? He might just be out there camping."

"Pull up now, Letty."

The man on the earth below them braced his feet wide apart and shaded his eyes with one hand to gaze up at them. In his other hand he held a gun.

"Oh my God," Sandra gasped. "Up, Letty. Go up."

She glanced over her shoulder. "Quit fussing, Sandra."

"A gun. He's got a gun."

Almost lazily, he lifted his pistol and took aim.

Letty yanked the throttle and they ascended like an elevator.

Below them, a second man joined the first. He was also armed. They might have been firing, but the whir of the helicopter covered any sound of a pistol's retort.

Sandra jostled back in her seat, shocked. Though McCloud and Pablo had mentioned rustlers and renegades, she hadn't given them much thought. When she remembered that first night, the danger of a campfire hadn't seemed real. What if these men had found them? What if, instead of Martin White Horse, she and McCloud had come face-to-face with these renegades?

"Mark this canyon," Pablo said. "When we get into Alamosa, we will tell my cousin the sheriff."

"Right," Sandra concurred. "Surely he can come out here and round these people up."

Letty wheeled toward a neighboring canyon, leaving the men and their guns behind.

"What will the sheriff do?" Sandra demanded. "Raise a posse?"

"Oh, sure." Pablo chuckled. "We gather up all the men in town and ride into the desert."

"Why is that funny? Obviously, these men are the rustlers and this is their hideout. The sheriff needs to apprehend them."

"But this isn't the Old West," McCloud said. "We're probably forty miles from Alamosa. The people in the town are shopkeepers, professors, accountants and even attorneys. They're not likely to form much of a posse."

"But they shot at us!"

McCloud shrugged. "No damage done."

She turned her head to glare at him, but they were too close, and his smile was too distracting. "If you don't take these men seriously, McCloud, nothing will be done about them. I'm willing to press charges."

"I'm with Sandra," Letty said. "I say we head for Alamosa and contact Pablo's cousin. Besides, I need fuel."

"I can't argue with that," McCloud said. "Let's head into town."

Sandra folded her arms below her breasts. This quest was far more complicated than she had anticipated. Reluctantly, she faced the fact that McCloud's tedious procedure of trooping up and down canyons was probably the only way to successfully cover the area. She'd underestimated him.

AT THE SMALL AIRPORT at Alamosa, Letty arranged for refueling and checked out the undercarriage of her helicopter to make sure none of the renegade bullets had found their mark. Then McCloud borrowed a Jeep, and they went to town. In Alamosa, they split up. Pablo and Letty went to do the marketing Elena had requested.

McCloud stepped up beside Sandra. "Lunch?"

"Thank you, but no."

Even to her own ears, the response sounded stiff and overly polite. There was an apology she needed to make to him, but the words stuck in her throat.

"Not hungry, Sandra?"

"That's not it. It's just that for the first half of this morning, I was regretting breakfast. I'd better keep my stomach relatively empty." She looked up quickly. "But if you'd like to eat, go ahead."

"I'd rather stretch my legs."

They strolled together down the two-lane main street in this sprawling town that was the center of commerce for the San Luis Valley and home of Adams State College. "And," McCloud informed her, "it's also the fungus capital of the world."

"I hope we're talking about mushrooms."

"Absolutely." He moved along the street at a casual, moseying pace. "Where did you grow up, Sandra? Big city?"

"We lived in Chicago for a while. But mostly, it was places like this."

A steady stream of trucks, cars and motorcycles whisked along the street where parking was diagonal at the curb, offering ready access to the shops, cafés, drugstores and bars. Sandra gave a reminiscent sigh. The small-town flavor tasted familiar to her.

When she was growing up, her family had lived in dozens of similar towns and, after a while, they'd become a fading montage of lazy streets and stray dogs and chipped paint. All the brave little towns, from Maine to California, where the people were friendly and the economy struggled. "I'm from every place," she said. "And no place."

Sandra had always been the outsider, the new girl in town. And, as she sauntered down this Alamosa street, she realized that she still was. McCloud, on the other hand, belonged here. Technically, it wasn't his residence, but with his Levi's and cowboy hat and moccasins he fit in. His startling turquoise eyes set him apart, but he was comfortable, at home. It would have been nice to link up with McCloud, to place her hand in his and draw reassurance from his solid broadshouldered presence, but that wouldn't be right. She'd drawn battle lines between them, lines that she now realized were somewhat misguided.

Sandra took a deep breath and glanced up at him. Might as well get this over with. "I guess I owe you an apology, McCloud."

"Why?"

"Because I haven't treated your search seriously. I figured it wasn't much more than a half-baked scheme, and I'm frankly surprised that you've done detailed maps and collected information on the legend in a meticulous and organized manner." She took another bite of humble pie. "I've been obnoxious, charging down here with a helicopter as if I'd just invented technology."

"You're right. And you're wrong."

"What does that mean?"

"You're dead right about your attitude."

"My obnoxiousness? Thank you, McCloud. You have no idea how sensitive that makes me feel."

"But you're wrong to think that you were totally off base. A lot of my search is because I enjoy meandering around the canyons."

He was being generous, and she appreciated his candor. "You know, McCloud, you might have saved us some trouble by mentioning ahead of time that a helicopter search was largely unproductive."

"You wouldn't have believed me."

"No, I suppose not."

They were back at the Jeep. "Let's take a ride," he said.

"Just leave Letty and Pablo here?"

"Trust me, Sandra. Elena has given them enough shopping to last another hour."

In the Jeep, they left the main drag and followed a two-lane downhill street. A few blocks from the business district, they passed a row of tired-looking frame houses. Though the lawns were green, there was an untended aura about them. In one neat yard, a flower garden added a splash of springtime color. Yellow crocus. Lavender iris.

"I can't help thinking there has to be an easier way," she said. "Searching those canyons could take eight more years."

"If I didn't enjoy the search itself, I would have quit long ago, Sandra."

"I don't get it. How can you stand to waste all that time?"

"I just told you that I was enjoying myself," he repeated patiently. "I'm having fun, in my own way."

"But it's so inefficient."

"Many pleasures are."

Outside the town, he parked in a pull-off beside a growth of cottonwoods. Sandra was aware of a new sound, a rushing. "Where are we?" she asked, as he preceded her out of the Jeep.

"Downstream. Where everything is easy."

"Don't be cryptic with me, McCloud. I like to know where I'm going, why and how long it will take."

"Then you're going to hate the next two weeks."

"What does that mean?"

"You'll have no schedules, no appointments, no secretaries." He indicated a path through the cottonwoods. "Some people call it a vacation, Sandra."

"Not me. Even on vacation, I have an itinerary."

They came through the trees to the river's bank where the waters roiled and shimmered in the sunlight. "The Rio Grande," he said.

She'd seen the river before. It was beautiful, but not impressive. Not like the mighty Mississippi or the wide Potomac. The Rio Grande was a tough river, feisty and swift. A piece of driftwood caught in the current and shot forward. Unstoppable. "Why did you bring me here?"

"No special reason." He lowered himself to the grassy bank and sat. "The river is a beginning, a source. Just lean back and enjoy. Think of where these waters are going, where they've been."

She sat beside him.

"Without this river, Sandra, the Southwest would be dead. There would be no irrigation, no growth, no vegetation. No people."

Her gaze was suspicious. "Are you sure there's no hidden meaning in coming here?"

"None. Nothing to imply or deduce or ponder." He grinned as he looked at her. "Can you live with that, Sandra?"

"I don't know." She leaned back on her elbows and tried to experience the river as being just a river, but her mind was too active. She fidgeted. "I hate this."

"Why?"

"It's not my nature to simply experience something. I like my actions to have purpose. I want my messages clear and my meanings defined."

"Always?"

"When I look at the Rio Grande, I want to know where it starts and where it will end."

He stretched his long legs toward the water, basking in the sound of rushing water. His deep voice harmonized with the river. "When we made love, Sandra, where did you think it would end?"

His words surprised her. She'd been struggling not to think of that night. Sudden confrontation with that memory caused tension to coil within her like the mainspring of a watch. Her mouth felt suddenly dry, and she licked her lips. She stammered a reply. "I wasn't really thinking. When we, um, when we made love, I didn't consider the consequences."

Obviously not, she told herself. Or she never would have done it.

"And now?"

An uncomfortable heat rose in her body, flushing her cheeks. In a rush, she said, "I guess if I'd considered the whole issue, I would have assumed that it would end right there. In the high desert. In that tent. No future."

"A one-night stand?"

She bristled. Not only did his statement sound appallingly tawdry, but it lacked the ring of truth. Sandra had never been the sort of woman who went for one-night stands. In relationships, she'd always protected herself with high standards. She never even kissed on a first date. "What are you getting at, McCloud?"

His turquoise eyes reflected the river. "That night. I've thought about it a lot. About you."

"And?"

He hesitated. "Don't misinterpret this, Sandra, but there was something fated in our lovemaking. I'm not saying that you're a reincarnation of Dawn Fire. Or that we were unconsciously fulfilling a modern version of the legend. But it wasn't a one-night stand. Not for me."

"The implications are..." Logic failed her. Surely, he wasn't talking about an ongoing relationship. Between him and her? Impossible! She couldn't even begin to consider that possibility. "Some clarification is needed here, McCloud. Let's keep in mind that I am here because my career demanded my presence."

"Your career?"

"Martin White Horse went to Laurence Jessop and told him about the legend. I'm here to find the city of gold."

"Do you believe the legend?"

"I believe a legend exists."

"Do you understand," he asked, gently, "that the heart of the legend is love? It's the story of a man and a woman, learning to follow their hearts."

"Love?" She bounced to her feet and vigorously dusted off her backside. Her gaze carefully avoided his. She couldn't stand to talk about deeper emotions while looking at him. "This surely is not about love, not by a long shot. Finding a city of gold is about greed."

"Is that why you're here? Greed?"

"That's why my parents invested with you," she said. "They thought they would get rich quick, that they'd find some pot of gold at the end of the rainbow."

"Not your mother."

"No, probably not. She's always been more enamored with the rainbow than the pot of gold. But I'm certain that when they dragged me into this, they weren't thinking about love."

Or perhaps they were. Perhaps her parents had hoped that by throwing Sandra and McCloud together, the two of them might connect. Perhaps that was why they'd had him give her the documents about their investment with McCloud. Oh, good grief, that was a ghastly thought! Getting sucked into one of her parents' roundabout, goofy plots? Sandra shook her head in vehement denial. "Not even Thornton and Emma would go to all that trouble. They wouldn't set up this whole elaborate scheme so I'd be forced to spend time with you. Would they?"

"Couldn't be." He stood beside her on the riverbank. "Your parents don't even know Martin White Horse, and he was instrumental in causing you to come back to me."

"To come back to you?"

She looked up at him. Her eyes recognized the fire that shone in his gaze. The dizzying rushing sound of the Rio Grande surrounded them, pulling her inexorably closer to him. She wanted to feel his arms holding her, his hands caressing her, the warmth of his mouth pressing against hers.

"We have a future, Sandra."

"No. We have a past." Desperately, she turned away from him. This couldn't be happening. She couldn't give in to the inappropriate physical urges of her body. "We made a mistake. *I* made a mistake."

"You know that's not true."

"But it is."

She pivoted and started up the path toward the Jeep. "We'd better get back. Letty and Pablo are surely done with the shopping by now. And while we're here, we really ought to talk with Pablo's cousin, the sheriff."

"For somebody who's so perceptive, Sandra, you're being blind."

In her haste, she stumbled over her own feet and fell to the ground. On her hands and knees, she shook her head, wanting to clear the confusion. The trees and open skies whirled around her. Her ears echoed with the sound of the river, and she imagined being dragged along by a swift current, drowning her doubts and her fears, helpless against the destiny McCloud kept insisting bonded their futures.

McCloud touched her shoulders. Gently he helped her up.

Instead of shaking away from him, she sought comfort, the warmth of his presence, the illogical sense of safety and shelter that she felt when he was near her. Nothing bad could touch her while he was there. No one could hurt her.

For one charmed moment, she allowed herself to succumb to the mesmerizing message in his turquoise gaze—the silent message of a man to a woman. Her breath came in short gasps. Her lips parted.

When he kissed her, Sandra thought she would die from the absolute rightness of the moment. She hadn't realized how much she had longed for him, for his kiss, for the heat of his body against hers.

"I can't," she murmured. But her hands clung to him. "McCloud, this isn't—"

"Not the place," he agreed. When he looked at her, his eyes burned right through her. "I can wait. Until tonight."

Chapter Eight

Until tonight? What was he planning?

The afternoon hours passed like slow sand through an hourglass. Another helicopter flight. Another dinner. This time, after eating, Sandra refused when McCloud asked her to come onto the porch and watch the sunset.

"Not tonight," she said, hoping he would catch the implication. *Not tonight!* Nothing else would happen between them tonight. Or any other night, for that matter.

"Are you tired?" McCloud asked. His eyes seemed to be asking other questions, more personal questions.

"Very tired." Sandra latched on to that excuse. "So exhausted that I can't imagine doing anything more strenuous than taking a bath and falling into bed."

She nodded to the other people sitting around the long dining room table. "Good night."

Letty and Pablo hardly noticed her impending departure. They were wrapped up in each other and anxious to be alone.

The other ranch hand who had shared their dinner ducked his head shyly and mumbled a "Good night, ma'am."

Elena, who had joined them for dinner, seemed lost in reverie, probably mentally preparing tomorrow's menu with the fresh supplies they'd purchased in Alamosa.

Only McCloud acknowledged Sandra when she rose from the table. He stood at his place—gentlemanly and proper, she thought suspiciously. What was going on in his mind? The uncertainty caused her heart to jump like a nervous jackrabbit. "Good night, McCloud."

"Pleasant dreams," he said.

Fat chance! How could she sleep when her mind was ripping through the possibilities with the frantic speed of a Cripple Creek slot machine. Ka-chink. Ka-chink. Ka-chink. Would she be a winner tonight? Or a loser? If luck were really a lady, there would be no question. They would not make love again. Ever.

But, oh, how she wanted him. She trudged down the hall to her bedroom. If he came to her tonight in her bedroom, she would send him away, would refuse to participate in the destiny he so believed in, the future he'd charted. Ka-chink! Or maybe not. Maybe she would listen to her body's yearnings and invite him into her bed. Ka-chink! Or what if he didn't come to her at all? What if he changed his mind? Ka-chink!

Stripping off her clothes, she went into the large bathroom between her room and Letty's. With a vicious flick of her wrist, she turned the faucets in the tub to scalding hot. A cloud of steam swirled ceilingward, and the moisture permeated her pores. A good long soak in the tub was what she needed. Keeping the water temperature as hot as she could stand it, Sandra slowly lowered her naked body into the water and sank to her nostrils, hoping to boil away these ridiculous desires for a man she hardly knew and had reason to distrust.

She submerged, holding her breath and taking the heat into every part of her body, then came out of the water, sucking in the cooler air of the room. Using a gardenia-scented shampoo she'd brought from Denver, she lathered her hair, rinsed it, washed it. Her cleansing process took on the meticulous attitude of a ritual as she used every toiletry item she'd packed: the loofah sponge on the roughened skin of her elbows and heels, three separate cleansing and moistening products on her face.

Though she'd intended to soak, her bath was completed with relative speed. Too quickly, her hair blew dry and the final dose of moisturizer sank into her skin. Wearing her soft cotton nightie, she opened the door of the bathroom and entered her Southwestern-style bedroom with the whole long night stretched out ahead of her.

During her bath, the sun had gone down, and the room was dark—except for the flicker of a single crimson candle on her bedside table. Beneath the pewter candle holder was a note. She recognized McCloud's bold handwriting: *Sandra, I'd like to see you tonight. If you agree, place this light in your window.*

"Oh, no." Her heart sank. He was leaving it up to her. Once again, she felt outmaneuvered. With this simple note, he assured himself that he wouldn't step into an argument. If she agreed to see him, she was effectively giving her consent. She had to admire his tactics. He was asking for a decision *before* he came to her.

A sigh trembled on her lips. It was so darned romantic. She ought to refuse, point-blank. But how could she?

She glanced at the window, half expecting that she would see him standing there, waiting. His presence was everywhere on this ranch and in these plains. The light breeze through the opened casement window whispered in his voice. Fragrant springtime air tingled against her warm skin.

Taking the candle and carefully shielding the flame with her cupped hand, she crossed the room. A sign? A signal? One if by land and two if by sea. She peered out into the silence of the night. A light from the barn cast long shadows and shimmered on the leaves of the cottonwood outside her window. Was he out there? Did he feel the same tension that she did?

Soon she would know. Sandra placed the lighted candle on the tiled window ledge.

When she slipped beneath the quilts in her overly soft and fluffy bed, an anxious sensation curled in her belly, and she almost bolted from the bed to blow out the candle. She didn't have to make love to him. This wasn't a signed contract. Putting a candle in the window did not obligate her to anything.

Still, it might be best not to greet him in bed. She pushed her way out of the soft mattress, threw on a robe and sat in the rocking chair beside the window. She waited, listening with all her might for the soundless approach of McCloud's moccasins on the hardwood floor outside her bedroom door.

Though the bedside clock showed an elapsed time of sixteen minutes, an eternity passed. The brass handle on her bedroom door turned slowly, slowly. Sandra's fingers clenched into fists. Her nipples hardened to tense peaks. The suspense was killing her.

Then the door opened. Light from the hallway silhouetted his wide shoulders.

"McCloud?" she whispered.

"I'm here, Sandra."

In the moonlight from the window, she saw him reach for the light switch beside the door. "Please don't," she said.

"But I wanted to see you."

And she wanted to hide, didn't want to show him how easily she might be seduced. Somehow, in the semidarkness, she felt as if they were more equal.

The door closed. He crossed the room and turned toward her. The candlelight played across the rugged planes of his face and gave a mysterious shimmer to his eyes. She could not doubt—not even for a moment—that she wanted to make love to this man. "Why did you want to see me, McCloud?"

"For a big-city woman like yourself, that's a naive question."

"Well, there could be dozens of reasons. To discuss our plans for the search. To explore insights into the legend of Dawn Fire. To admit that you were wrong about the contracts." She paused to catch her breath. Her barrage of words echoed in the room. "Why, McCloud?"

On silent feet, he approached the rocking chair where she sat. His face was in shadow. "Lady, I want to make love to you."

His hand stroked her cheek, descended her throat. She could feel him trembling as he caressed her.

Sandra knew that she ought to stop him. *Stop him now!* It wasn't fair to either of them to allow this charade to continue. "You'd better leave," she said. "We're going to be spending a lot of time together over the next few weeks, and this will only make us uncomfortable."

"I'm uncomfortable now," he said. "Every time I look at you, I want you."

"Be sensible, McCloud." There was undeniable passion between them. But not love. Not true caring. "We can't."

His lips nuzzled her hair. "You smell wonderful."

"Thank you, I think." When she attempted to stand, she was entrapped in his embrace. In a single motion, he lifted her and carried her to the bed. He set her down and joined her. Their combined weight caused them to wallow in the softness of the bed. The soft quilts and blankets tangled around them.

And Sandra laughed. Inside her, the brittle tension shattered like glass.

He struggled to a sitting position. "Damn this bed. I'd forgotten—"

"I've been meaning to talk to you about the mattress."

"It's goose down. One of Pablo's aunts or cousins manufactured the damn thing. It's warm as hell in the winter. But it's like sleeping underwater." He climbed out of the bed and held out his hand to help her. "This won't work. Let me take you to my bed, Sandra."

"No," she said. Though she was struggling in goose down, she managed to keep her resolve firm. "You're not going to come in here and seduce me just like that."

"And how do you want me to seduce you?"

"I'll let you know." She climbed ungracefully from the bed. "There are a few points that need clarification."

He groaned.

"In the library." She went to the window. "First, I should blow out this candle."

"Wish it was that easy," he muttered.

She lifted the pewter candle holder. She held it for a moment between them. "This was very clever," she said. "Why exactly did you leave me a note?"

"I didn't want to fight you."

"And if I had blown the candle out?"

"I would have spent a very long night in a very cold shower. Then, tomorrow I would have tried again."

He gazed fondly at her. Moonlight from the window glistened on the perfect oval of her face. They would make love again, he thought. Tonight. In the comfort of his own bed. "Let's go."

"To the library," she repeated. "There's something I've been thinking about in those accounts of the legend."

They padded through the silent hallways of the ranch house. McCloud's bedroom was at the far end, to the left of the library. He almost dragged her there when she stopped at the library door. This insistence on discussing the legend was an unusual bit of foreplay, McCloud thought, but he was held in thrall by his desire for her. If she'd demanded a dog and pony show, he would be out finding poodles and Shetlands.

In the library, she flicked on the overhead light as she entered. "The basic information in those legends was similar, but the maiden had many different names.

And all of those names had some kind of sky reference.''

"And the choice of her name seems to reflect the time imagery used in each legend," he said. "If her name is Dawn Fire, her departure occurs in the morning. If she is Star Flame, she leaves at night."

He had analyzed those legends, front to back and sideways. Over a period of months, he'd traveled to different tribes and sought out the most venerable storyteller of each to repeat the legend of the cities of gold. Then he'd recorded their stories on tape and had them transcribed.

But this was the first time he'd had the opportunity to discuss the manuscripts with someone who had taken the trouble to read each one. Though passion raged within him, this conversation promised to be interesting. He settled in one of the chairs at the map table and stretched out his legs. "What else did you notice, Sandra?"

"Is there one single legend that you would say is the true story?"

"Not really."

"But there must have been a source," she said. "One original story that spread and was adapted to each tribe."

"The source for folk tales is impossible to trace. It's one of the intrigues of anthropology. Why is it that so many cultures all over the world have similar stories? Was there one great source? Is there a universal unconscious that plays through the minds of all humankind? Or is it coincidence?"

She frowned at that idea.

"Reasonable coincidence," he said. "Several cultures in similar levels of development with similar concerns might have need of similar stories."

"Need?" she questioned.

"Like making love," he said gently.

"But all these stories aren't about that particular need." He noticed a blush on her cheek. "Are they?"

"No. Curiosity is a need, too. People have a need to make sense of their surroundings. As Joseph Campbell pointed out, there seems to be a universal need for heroes. And every individual has a need to achieve heroic stature in the context of his or her own life."

"And the theme of these stories," she said. "It might be related to some kind of sun worship. Like the Aztecs."

She perched on the edge of the table, near enough to him that he could reach over and touch her thigh, and he was mightily tempted to do so. She was so damn adorable that he had a hard time concentrating on her words. "Like the Aztecs," he repeated.

"There was the wonderful exhibit at the Denver Museum of Natural History," she said. "Did you see it?"

He nodded. "Yes, it was fascinating. The cities of gold played a tragic part in the death of that culture. The Spaniards believed literally in real golden spires and loot."

"And what do you think?"

"Golden cities are a metaphor for a beautiful, perfect life-style. Like a golden age. I think the cities of gold meant an era of peaceful development where there was a lack of strife and an abundance of good weather."

She idly picked up one of the maps on the table. "With all of these overhead photos, what were you looking for?"

"Nothing really. I just wanted a fairly accurate map of the area. I can't use the maps to eliminate areas that don't seem to fit the legend description of water and berries because vegetation and even the course of rivers can change over the centuries."

"Do you think there's a sign?" she asked. "An omen?"

"You mean like those mysterious circles that get tramped out in wheat fields?"

"Kind of. Some evidence, you know."

"Of what? Aliens?" Though McCloud tried to keep an open mind on most subjects, he couldn't believe some of the outrageous postulations on the fate of the Anasazi. "There's one theory that the whole tribe was carried off by aliens from another planet. Which, I guess, makes as much sense as the idea that the people of ancient Atlantis were turned into dolphins."

"Sounds like my mother," she said.

"What always amazes me about these strange theories is how people who believe them can manufacture a ton of evidence to support their view. They conjure up facts. Their logic is easily manipulated."

She frowned, taken aback. "Logic, McCloud, is my life."

"But it's not truth." He continued, "Truth comes from the heart. I can only follow a dream. When I see my destiny, I go after it."

"Not always," she murmured. "You didn't go after me like that. You left the decision to me, leaving the candle in my room."

"But I knew you couldn't refuse me. Not forever. Because I know, Sandra, that you want me as much as I want you. Our lovemaking is incredible and special. I wanted you to acknowledge that, to accept it."

Though he sounded confident now, McCloud hadn't been sure that she was ready to welcome him. When he'd left the red candle in her bedroom, he had heard the sounds of her bathing and had to force himself to leave her room, to hold back his own passion until she was ready. In the yard outside her window, he'd waited. And doubts ran cold in his blood. When he saw the candle in the window, the faint illumination on her face and hands, he'd held his breath. Would she blow it out?

Then she'd left it there, a beacon to guide him. And he'd been filled with pure joy. In the dark of night, there had seemed to be a glow. In the silence, the meadowlarks had seemed to be singing.

He reached toward her. His hand touched her firm thigh and lightly stroked the soft velour of her robe. The front gaped open and through the fine cotton of her gown, the rosy aureoles of her breasts beckoned to him. When their eyes met, he saw the desire she felt for him.

His voice sounded husky, even to him. "Your logic might have told you to refuse me."

"It does. There's no possibility of a relationship between us. Not a lasting relationship, and we can't—"

"Logic is a fool."

Standing, he took her hand and gave a subtle tug. She floated to him and he held her tight against his chest. He would possess this woman. "Sandra, my bed is wide and waiting."

"Show me."

Together, they left the library. He turned out the lights. His bedroom was right next door. There was an oil lamp beside his bed, casting a golden romantic shimmer.

"Is that light for me?" she asked.

"All light is yours. You are the source of brightness."

She folded herself against him. His hand played across her back.

"I think of you in a gentler time, Sandra. Another era. The time before harsh electricity." He tipped back her head. Her face was beautifully lit by the oil lamp glow. "I like seeing you in this light."

"Not as an aggressive feminist attorney?" she teased.

"Strong women aren't a problem for me," he said. "My Ute grandmother was a matriarch. My mother was an educated career woman in this area where it was unusual for women to do more than tend the house and care for their children." He pushed a wing of shining blond hair away from her face. "I like women who are strong and determined."

"You're a surprising man, McCloud."

They kissed. Her hands were low on his body, and he directed her fingers to the last button on his Levi's. She touched his hard arousal and her fingers drew back, shyly. Her instincts simultaneously warned her and urged her to make love with him.

She took a step backward and surveyed his bedroom. Like the rest of the house, the proportions were spacious. What she could see of the colors, in the soft glow of his lamp, were earth tones. The furniture loomed heavy and sturdy. His king-size bed, covered with the largest Navajo blanket she'd ever seen, had a huge carved frame.

Grasping for another topic while she keyed her desire from fever pitch to a more reasonable level, she went to the bedside and felt the texture of the soft wool blanket. "Is it handwoven?"

"Yes."

"It must be worth a small fortune."

"Not anymore. It's been washed and used for years and years. Some of the colors are faded." He came up behind her. "At my father's hardware store in Alamosa, he sometimes took handmade Native American objects in trade for goods and services."

"Clever man," she said, still keeping her back turned to McCloud "He must have amassed a fabulous collection."

"That wasn't why he did it. He was a shopkeeper, taking trades instead of cash because there wasn't much money. We used the pots for cooking and the rugs for covering the floor. An archaeologist who came out here for a visit pitched a fit about the rug on the floor in your bedroom. He said we should have hung it in a museum, that it was valuable."

"I'm sure he was right."

"That rug was payment for a toilet we installed at Carol Small Bird's house. Its value to us was as a rug."

"A matter of perspective," she said.

He stood directly behind her, and the whisper of his warm breath teased the nape of her neck as he continued their conversation. "Perspective. Like one man's hovel is another man's castle."

"One woman's dream is another woman's nightmare." She started to turn toward him, but he caught her shoulders holding her in position, facing away from him. "McCloud! What are you doing?"

"Tell me, Sandra." He slipped the velour robe from her shoulders. It fell to the floor and he kicked it aside. "Tell me about one woman's dream."

Sandra made a pretense at keeping up her end of their chat, as if she weren't being transported to the very edge of madness by his nearness. "In my line of work, I'm much more familiar with nightmares. People don't call an attorney when everything is going well."

"I would," he said. "I'd call you."

"Whatever for?"

"This."

He placed his hands on either side of her waist. He was still standing behind her, and when he fitted her buttocks against his thighs, his erection throbbed against her. Her breath caught sharply, but she managed to say. "*This?* People don't usually call an attorney for this."

"I'd call you whether you were an attorney or a housemaid or a goddess."

She reached back with both hands, grasping for him. With a pleased shock, she realized that he was naked, that somewhere between the door and the bed, he'd removed his jeans and his shirt. His hands glided up her torso to fondle her breasts.

"Sandra, you are my dream."

"No," she weakly protested. "I can't be."

His lips found the sensitive nape of her neck. He held aside her hair to nibble at the lobe of her ear. And, all the time, his fingers were doing amazing things to her breasts, raising the level of her excitement until her knees were weak.

His hands were at her waist again, bunching up the fabric of her nightie until he grasped the hem and slowly glided the smooth cotton up and over her raised arms.

When he turned her in his arms to kiss her full on the lips, their nude bodies pressed together, and the warmth within her became an inferno.

He tossed aside the magnificent Navajo blanket and guided her between the fresh-smelling, navy blue sheets. "I've imagined this," he said. "The way you'd look in my bed."

She was more perfect than his fantasies. Her creamy flesh made a magnificent contrast with his dark sheets, and her hair, her tousled blond hair, emitted a delicious scent. Her chestnut eyes implored him to touch her, to come closer. When she reached for him, he felt the strength in her grasp. Her body was trembling. Her lips parted, gasping for breath.

McCloud knew it would be difficult not to capitulate to the fever of lust that she heightened with each movement of her body. But he was determined to wait until she experienced the most complete orgasm of her life.

He kissed her hard, bruising her lips, and when he was done, she trembled against him.

"Oh," she gasped as he nibbled at her throat.

Sandra's desire built rapidly. She wanted him to claim her now, to feel him moving inside her again, but he proceeded with maddening slowness. His mouth was on her breast, flicking the hardened nipple. Then his kisses trailed down her belly.

Gently he parted her legs. Kneeling between her thighs, he lowered his head.

Sandra threw back her arms on the pillows as his tongue caressed her. Her body convulsed with dreadful, wonderful pleasure. She was completely out of control, awash in sensation. And he continued.

When, finally, his body poised above her, she clung to him, demanding with every fiber of her body that he fulfill her as a man completes a woman.

His first thrust was deliciously slow, and she pressed herself urgently against him.

"Slowly," he whispered.

"No," she cried. "I want you now."

"I can't hold back much longer," he said.

"Then don't. Please, don't."

But he did. His long slow thrusts stimulated her more than she believed was possible. Sandra heard a frenzied gasping, almost a sob, before she realized that the sounds were coming from her own throat.

At the moment when she thought she would die from pleasure, he struck deep and hard into the soft core of her arousal.

Her arms and legs went limp. Her heart soared, and pure sensation flooded her like a dam burst, melting her in a final sweet orgy of sheer delight.

It was several minutes before she could move or even open her eyes. When she did, McCloud was beside her, gazing down at her with the most arrogant expression she'd ever seen.

Though speaking was an effort, she licked her dry lips and forced out the words. "You're pretty proud of yourself."

"I am."

She sighed. "Well, you should be."

"What would you like to drink? Champagne? Wine? Nectar?"

"Milk," she said. Nothing sounded better than a tall cold glass of milk. "With ice cubes in it."

He gave her a quick kiss and moved from the bed. "I'll be right back. Anything else? Something to eat?"

"Something sweet."

"Your wish is my command."

He slipped back into his Levi's, and she'd never seen anything more sexy than McCloud buttoning his naked self into his jeans. A dangerous sense of possessiveness played at the edge of her thoughts. How could she ever leave this man?

When he left the room, she banished those considerations from her mind. Like Scarlett O'Hara, she would think about that tomorrow. And she would hope that an answer would appear on the horizon, glistening and right as a city of golden promise.

Chapter Nine

McCloud returned to his bedroom, carrying a small tray containing a glass of milk and a bowlful of chocolate chips. He whipped open the door and closed it behind him. "Here you are, madam. Milk and chocolate-chip cookies without the dough."

Sandra was already asleep. Her arms were sprawled artlessly across the pillows, and her legs were tangled in the sheets. Naked, she was magnificent.

He didn't wake her. Instead, he guzzled the milk and slipped beneath the sheets beside her. Careful not to rouse her, he straightened the blankets and stretched out on his back with his hands folded behind his head.

Their lovemaking had been everything he'd expected—and more. Better than he remembered, better than a fantasy. Sandra was so responsive. Her body was like a finely made violin, a Stradivarius, and it had been his privilege to pluck the strings.

He grinned. Amazing. The question now was how to get her to stay with him at the ranch longer than two weeks. He needed time to know her, to discover all her random thoughts and the nuances of her lovely body. And then . . . what?

Marry the woman?

No way, McCloud contradicted himself. She'd never consent to giving up her career. Living here, on a buffalo ranch, there wouldn't be enough to do. She'd be bored, dissatisfied, cranky.

On the other hand, there was no reason why she couldn't practice law here. There was a need for good attorneys in this vast land where jurisdictions were often confused and outlaws were hard to capture. She'd already heard Pablo's comments about the hassles in prosecuting the local renegades and rustlers.

Though it was incongruous to imagine the lovely Sandra in rural jailhouses and courtrooms, he guessed that she'd have Pablo's cousin and many of the other local sheriffs whipped into shape in no time. She'd probably get into politics, probably be a state senator. Why not? One of the United States senators, Ben Nighthorse Campbell, came from this part of the country. Tomorrow he'd point that out to her. She could have a career, a brilliant career, right here.

In her sleep, she shifted positions, snuggling against his chest with a soft purring sound. He tucked his arm around her. When he looked down at her face, her skin glowing in the lamplight, she seemed to be smiling.

"You're happy," he said softly. "Don't get me wrong, darlin'. I won't insist on slipping a wedding ring on your finger. But I want you to stay."

She mumbled something incoherent, and cuddled closer.

"Maybe not forever," he whispered, "but awhile. A good long while."

THE NEXT MORNING, when Sandra woke, she found herself wrapped around McCloud. One of her arms stretched across his broad chest, and her leg was flung over his. Memories of the night before flooded her mind and she sighed with utter contentment.

He was a marvelous lover. Not that she'd had a tremendous amount of experience to judge from, but she knew when she'd been well and truly satisfied. It must be one terrific afterglow if it had lasted all night and stayed with her into the dawn.

Gradually she moved her leg, not wanting to disturb him. Her thigh, she realized, had a pleasant sort of ache from their lovemaking. She disentangled her arm. Her breasts were warm and a little sore.

She lay quietly on her back, becoming reacquainted with her body. She was a different woman this morning, a woman who had explored the depths of her own passion and survived. Like a pioneer? She giggled at her own self-satisfaction.

But what came next? Tomorrow was already here, and there were decisions to be made about her new relationship with McCloud. But she had two weeks, didn't she? That would be plenty of time.

And then there was the whole city of gold thing. The thought crossed her mind that she might convince McCloud to forget the search for the next two weeks and simply stay here with her, making love all day and all night. But that wouldn't be right. She'd promised to search, and search she would. However, Sandra had no intention of trudging through the hillsides, eating dried buffalo meat and sleeping on the hard desert rocks. Nobody said that a quest had to be miserable.

With a fresh sense of purpose, she dragged herself from his bed and fumbled around on the floor until she located her nightie. She pulled it over her head, remembering how the fabric had taken on a life of its own when McCloud had massaged her.

She returned to his bedside and gazed down upon him. A very light stubble roughened his tanned cheeks. His black hair tumbled across his forehead. The navy blue sheet covered his lower body, but his chest and arms left much to be admired. She stared at the powerful juncture of muscle and bone, the thick pelt of black chest hair and the swarthy texture of his skin. Even at rest his hands, their fingers slightly curled, looked strong. As did the rest of his body.

Though tempted to pull back the sheet and make love to him in the early-morning light, Sandra grabbed her robe, crept from his bedroom and hurried barefoot down the hardwood floors toward her room.

From the end of the hall, she heard Elena already beginning her breakfast preparations, and Sandra made a detour to the kitchen.

"*Buenos días,* Elena. Is there coffee?"

"*Sí.*" Her dark eyes followed Sandra. "Did you have a good night?"

"Oh, yes." Did she know? Would the whole ranch be snickering behind their hands? "Why do you ask?"

"The mattress in your room. It is not so comfortable."

"I slept well." Sandra went to the huge stainless-steel urn and twisted the tap to shoot hot coffee into her mug. The dark brew was thick and rugged, like everything else around this place, and she winced at her first sip.

Elena laughed. "The coffee? It is strong?"

"Strong? This is the Arnold Schwarzenegger of coffees."

"The men like it. So this is how I make it."

"But you don't drink this yourself, do you?"

"I usually settle for tea."

"But do you like coffee?"

"Good Colombian coffee? *Sí*. But I don't even bother to buy the beans anymore. It is wasteful to brew a whole pot for the little bit that I drink."

Sandra forced down another gulp. "I think, Elena, that we should reeducate the men on what coffee should taste like."

"They are stubborn," she warned. "Especially McCloud."

"I know."

He was stubborn and demanding and ... altogether wonderful, in his way. Sandra left the dregs of her coffee in the kitchen and went to her bedroom where she peeled off her nightie, showered and dressed. A new, vigorous energy coursed through her and she couldn't wait to get into action.

All dressed and clean, she tapped on the door to Letty's bedroom. "Letty, are you awake?"

"Go away."

Sandra pushed open the door. With obnoxious cheerfulness, she announced, "It's morning."

"If you turn on the light..." Her words were slow. "I will kill you."

"Out late last night? Did you have a good time?"

"Sandra, I'm in no mood for girl talk. Pablo is one helluva a man. I like him. Lots. And that is all she wrote."

"Okay." Sandra picked her way out of the room. "As soon as you can drag yourself out of the sack, I've got plans."

"Peachy keen."

While she was playing the uncharacteristic role of happy-good-morning pixie, Sandra decided to flit into McCloud's room. She stood at the door, wondering if she should knock or not. Not after last night, she decided.

She peeked inside. He was still in bed, propped up on his pillows. A weekly newsmagazine was open on his lap, and he wore his reading glasses, which he immediately removed to shoot her a turquoise gaze that was so hot and sexy, her legs turned to Jell-O.

"You're up," she said idiotically.

"Come here, Sandra."

She closed the door but stayed beyond the range of his grasp. If he touched her, she knew that she would not resist, she'd tumble into his arms.

And what was so wrong with that?

"I have plans for today," she announced.

"So do I." Suggestively, he raised an eyebrow and patted the vacant space on his king-size bed. "Come here and let me tell you all about them."

Instinctively, she kept away from him. It would be easy to fall into his bed and never leave. But she would be giving up all control if she allowed him to call all the shots. "We're looking for the city of gold," she said. "Right?"

"Sandra, we're not going to spend another day swooping around in the helicopter. It's really a futile exercise."

Today she was calling the shots. "Well, we are taking a trip in the helicopter. But not to search the canyons."

"No?"

She went to the door and opened it. Brightly, she said, "We're going to Santa Fe."

WITHIN THE HOUR, Letty and Pablo had taken their places at the breakfast table. Their smoldering glances were hotter than the jalapeños in Elena's breakfast burritos.

Sandra didn't bother them with her plans until McCloud was seated at the head of the table. He gazed at her and asked, "Santa Fe?"

"Letty, how long would it take to fly to Santa Fe?"

"Dunno. A couple of hours." She tore her gaze away from Pablo to ask, "Why are we going to Santa Fe?"

"The search by helicopter up and down canyons is largely unproductive." She surveyed their affirmative responses. "So we obviously need to set out on horseback. And I have already experienced, firsthand, McCloud's idea of a luxurious camp-out. I need to purchase some equipment."

"Equipment?" McCloud's tone was rough, probably a result of drinking that sludge he called coffee. "Sandra, I saw the amount of luggage you packed, and there's no way we can take that much junk. I'm not going to load down the packhorse."

"But I'm not like you, McCloud. I can't wear the same pair of jeans for four days. I need supplies. And I want to go to Santa Fe to get them."

"Hold it." McCloud massaged his temples. "At the risk of being a dense, dirty male, why Santa Fe? There are sporting-goods stores in Alamos and Raton."

"I want the variety offered by a good-size city." Sandra knew she was being unreasonable, but it somehow felt right to give him a hard time, to let him know that she wasn't a pushover, that she would not be easily dominated. Demanding a trip to Santa Fe to shop felt . . . feminine. "I want to buy the best. I can afford it. And I deserve it. You don't have to come if you don't want to."

"Oh, I'm coming," he said. "Because there's no way I'm letting you buy a ton of stuff that we can't take with us anyway."

"I think it's a great plan," Letty said. "There's a café down there that has chicken enchiladas to die for."

McCloud and Pablo exchanged a glance and shook their heads simultaneously.

"*Mujeres*," Pablo muttered. "*Son locas.*"

Letty turned to Sandra. "What did he say?"

"Women," Sandra translated. "They're crazy."

"Well, Pablo, you can pack up your cute little *hasta la vista*." Letty pushed away from the table. "Because we're going to Santa Fe. Departure is in ten minutes. Sandra, bring your credit cards."

Sandra enjoyed this flight considerably more than the last one. Not only did her stomach feel better, but she enjoyed sitting in the back next to McCloud. Though he hadn't completely accepted the idea of her shopping excursion, he was attentive and polite. A few minutes away from the ranch, he looked down and pointed. "There's the bulk of the herd."

Letty slowed to a hover, high enough overhead that she didn't spook the grazing buffalo.

Sandra beamed with delight at the sight of all those huge shaggy beasts, roaming free. This was the legacy of the Old West, almost destroyed by the coming of the settlers and the wholesale slaughter of the buffalo. She was proud that McCloud was somehow responsible for reintroducing this animal to the high desert plains. "How many head?" He'd told her before, but she couldn't remember.

"Nearly a couple thousand, not including the calves."

"Why do you count the calves separately?"

"Because they're not salable. And some of them don't make it."

"How sad," Letty said.

"That's the way nature is," Sandra commented. "Nothing to be sad or angry about. That's life. Some make it, and some don't."

"Unusual attitude for a city girl," McCloud said.

"I grew up in rural towns."

And she'd learned not to grow too attached to the cute little piggies and baby chicks and calves. Raising meat was the way of farming, her parents had told her. But Sandra hadn't believed them. She thought they were being cruel, denying her any attachment, keeping her from having any friendships, not even with an animal. And then her favorite piglet had grown to edibility and had been shipped off to slaughter. After that, she'd never had a pet. No attachments meant no pain.

She needed to keep that in mind, especially in her dealings with McCloud. No attachments.

Letty moved into forward gear and they left the herd behind. As they continued, McCloud pointed out the local landmarks. Ship Rock. Eagle's Nest. "We're roughly following the Santa Fe trail," he said. "Over Raton Pass."

"People did this in covered wagons?"

"And I'll bet they wore their jeans longer than four days."

"Only because they didn't have helicopters and credit cards."

In Santa Fe, Sandra hired a compact rental car and drove toward the center of the town, the adobe square outside the Governor's Palace where the natives displayed jewelry, pottery and a variety of wares on the sidewalk.

McCloud sank down in the passenger seat while Sandra drove. "This is the tourist section of town," he said. "I thought you needed camping gear."

"But the really good restaurant," Letty said, "is right down here. Turn left at the next corner."

After a few more lefts and a right, Letty had found her special place, which looked to McCloud like any one of a dozen small adobe cafés with tables on an outside patio.

His impatience had begun to simmer. There was a game being played here, and he wasn't too sure about the rules. He wanted to get Sandra alone for a few minutes, to find out the real reason behind this apparently senseless excursion.

"Tell you what," he said, holding open the car door for Letty and Pablo. "We'll do Sandra's shopping for camping equipment, and pick you up back here in a couple of hours."

Not listening to objections, he dropped them on the curb and waved goodbye. Pablo looked particularly forlorn, but that couldn't be helped. If his ranch foreman insisted upon getting hooked by a big blond pilot with an appetite, that was his problem. McCloud had enough to worry about. He turned to Sandra. "Drive."

"But I don't know where we're—"

"Straight down this road to the next main intersection."

They pulled away and Sandra stuck her cute little nose into the air. "Aren't we cranky?"

"Yes, we are." He tried to stretch out his legs, but it was impossible in the small car. He was certain she'd rented the compact to make him uncomfortable. "Mind telling me what the hell is going on?"

"I explained once. I'm shopping for supplies."

McCloud tugged the brim of his hat lower on his brow. "I understand that. Actually, it makes sense for you to take along stuff that will make the trip easier for you. But that isn't why we're here, is it?"

She was approaching a stoplight. "Left or right?"

"Right."

He waited until they were in the parking lot of a large shopping mall. The style, like most of the buildings in Santa Fe, was adobe. When Sandra reached for her door handle, he grasped her arm. "Why?"

"Because I want to." Her chin jutted stubbornly. "In spite of what happened last night, I have my own ideas, my own plans and my own goals."

"I don't get it, Sandra. Are we going shopping so that you can assert your independence?"

"In a way."

"And what if I asked you to stay with me?"

"I've already agreed to stay for two weeks."

"What if I wanted more of your time?"

She wasn't sure what he was asking, and she chose to be flippant rather than to take him seriously. "I guess I'd have to bill you at my regular hourly rate. And I warn you, McCloud, I'm not cheap."

"Give me a month."

"I can't stay, McCloud. I can't."

Sandra couldn't begin to think of that possibility. She had a career, a full-time life, and it was back in

Denver. How could she stay here? It wasn't as if she and McCloud were in love. They were nothing more than two consenting adults who had shared a night of passion. An incredible night. But she couldn't chart her life based on great sex.

"Do you understand?" she asked.

"Not at all," he said. His hands rose and fell in a gesture of pure exasperation. "You dragged all of us down here to Santa Fe in a helicopter because you wanted to make it clear to me that you aren't planning to spend your life with me. Right?"

"Maybe."

"But I thought you were supposed to be so logical." He tried to twist his body in the small compact car to face her, but there was no natural way for him to maneuver his shoulders and legs into the right position. Frustrated, he sank back in the dinky bucket seat. "Why shopping?"

"It's a female thing," she snapped. "Out there on the range, you're in your environment. You're in control. But here—" she gestured toward the mall "—here, I'm the boss. You're out of your element."

"So this is a control thing?"

She grinned. "I have this lovely mental image of you trailing behind me, carrying dozens of packages. I want to take you to lingerie departments and watch you squirm."

He shuddered. "Why?"

"Because I can. Because you'll do it. Even though you don't want to, you'll humor me." She laughed at the utterly perplexed look on his face. "Come on, cowboy, let's shop."

He escorted her into an upscale department store where a cute young thing scampered up to them and insisted upon spritzing McCloud with an atomizer of a brand-new cologne. A masculine fragrance, she called it.

His nose wrinkled. He scowled dangerously, and the cologne lady moved away from them.

At the sporting-goods store, Sandra found a full-size pop-open tent that compressed to a small duffel bag, a double-size air mattress with pump, a battery-operated coffeemaker and heated socks.

She experimented with a battery-operated blow dryer.

"No," McCloud said gruffly.

She glanced over her shoulder at him and added the dryer to her stack of potential purchases.

"We can't carry all that," he said.

"So we bring another horse."

"You don't get it, Sandra. The idea here is to travel light, to cover a lot of ground."

"That might be *your* idea," she replied, "but I'm going to be as prepared and comfy as possible."

"We'll never be more than a day's ride from the ranch," he protested. "If we run into problems, we can always get back."

"Don't let me forget the cellular phone."

There were four different lamps that she checked over, trying to decide which would provide the most light.

"Not another lamp." Exasperation was evident in his voice. "We don't want to—"

"I know. We don't want to signal our position." She replaced the lamp and turned to the clerk who had formed a permanent attachment to her. "I'd like to look at guns, please."

McCloud groaned. "I have guns. You don't need guns."

She smiled at the clerk. "Knives, then. I'm sure I can use a sturdy hunting knife."

When she was done, Sandra had rigged a belt with a hunting knife, a Swiss army knife, a compass, a canteen, a flare gun and an emergency first-aid kit. When she walked, she rattled. "And I still have all these little loops to hang things from," she said.

"No more," he pleaded. "You already look like a giant charm bracelet."

She added a couple more items of rain gear and proceeded across the store to the clothing section where she found three pairs of thermal underwear and several pairs of wool and cotton socks. After trying on a variety of sizes and styles, she selected a pair of flexible-sole hiking boots.

That was all for the sporting-goods store. "But there's the whole rest of the mall," she said with an evil grin. "And we'll need food. Especially coffee."

He didn't object to her purchase of a mobile phone, but he drew the line at a notebook-size computer and fax. "What the hell are you planning to do? File legal briefs from the high desert?"

"I might want to. I have a career, you know."

"Hell, yes. I'm real damn aware of your career."

"Good. Because that career is why I'm stuck with this trek into the desert."

"Just forget it, Sandra. You don't have to come with me. As a matter of fact, I don't want you to come with me."

"You should have thought of that before you sent Martin White Horse to my law firm."

"I didn't—" He threw his hands in the air. "Forget I said anything. I'll follow behind you. I'll carry your packages. Let's just get this over with. All right?"

"Certainly," she said sweetly. "Oh, look. There's a sale at Victoria's Secret."

A short while later, when they finally returned to pick up Letty and Pablo, the restaurant manager informed McCloud that their friends had decided to return to the square.

"Swell," McCloud muttered. "Now we're going to have to fight through the crowds to find them."

"Shouldn't be too difficult," Sandra pointed out. "Letty in her hot pink jumpsuit kind of stands out. Besides, it's a shame to come to Santa Fe and not browse."

At the square, she expertly picked her way through the sidewalk vendors, separating the truly artistic jewelry from the junk. There was one necklace that appealed to her. Inlaid turquoise on a silver thunderbird. She asked the name of the artist, and the woman who was tending the sidewalk display handed her a card.

With a flick of her fingernail, Sandra tapped the familiar name. "One of my mother's students."

"He's pretty good," McCloud said.

"Very good. And, from this address, it looks like he's got himself a little studio. I guess he's successful."

"Like your mother?"

She looked up with surprise. Sandra didn't really think of her mother as being a success as an artist. But, of course, she was. Emma Carberry sold consistently. Several galleries displayed her work, and her agent demanded a decent price for her paintings. "I guess she is a success."

"Takes a hell of a lot of determination to make it as an artist," McCloud said. "Not to mention talent. You must be proud of her career."

Her career? Sandra didn't think of her mother that way. Emma was the irresponsible, flaky person who couldn't quite get dinner on the table. She was the mother who forgot PTA meetings and Brownie field trips and the awards banquet for the speech meet when Sandra and her partner had won first prize in debate. It seemed impossible, but perhaps Emma was, like Sandra herself, very much caught up in her career.

"You're like her," he said.

"Hard to believe. We never agreed on anything. Even when I was trying to be cooperative, we were always at odds."

"But not on the important things," he said. "Like feminism."

"Or world peace. Or environmentalism. Of course not."

The play of soft sunlight on adobe walls made long shadows. It was growing late, and Sandra closed her eyes in a slow blink. Why had her mother decided to have children? Sandra and her brother and sister must have been a detriment to Emma's career as an artist. They slowed her down. And yet, she'd never seemed resentful. Forgetful, perhaps, but not hostile toward them. She'd always loved them.

"Maybe we helped," she said. "Maybe my mother needed us to complete her vision of life."

"And maybe," McCloud said, "children were the natural product of her love for your father."

There was that factor to consider. Love. Throughout her childhood and growing up, Sandra had known love. She'd been lonely, but she had been loved. In her adult life, love was sadly missing.

She linked arms with McCloud and they strolled slowly until they found Pablo and Letty.

"We'd better head back," Letty said. "I need to get back to Denver by tomorrow noon."

"And we need to make an early start," McCloud said. "Tomorrow at dawn."

"So early?" Sandra squeaked.

"Yes. And, lucky for us, you have an alarm clock attached to your pedometer to keep track of the time as well as the distance we're going to travel."

She knew there would be many minutes and miles before she made sense of all these questions. Her parents. Love. And McCloud.

They flew back to the ranch through a sunset.

Chapter Ten

That night he came to her again.

But it wasn't the same. The night before, McCloud had been the perfect lover. The dark that wrapped around them had been lit by the flickering glow of a crimson taper, signaling the warmth of desire.

Tonight, McCloud tapped on her door and entered, carrying three large saddlebags, which he dropped with a thud onto the hardwood floor. "This is all the packing space you have. Not including the tent."

Sandra didn't know whether to laugh or cry. This wasn't what she expected from McCloud. Not after dark, anyway. Pasting a noncommittal smile on her face, she responded, "I can't fit everything in there. What about the air mattress and pump?"

"Fit them in or leave them behind." He squared his shoulders. "You bought too much junk. I told you—"

"Please don't say, 'I told you so.'"

"I won't. But I did."

"I hate that," she said. "It's so smug. And I don't deserve it. Not when I'm being such a good sport about this whole thing."

"Why is that?" He slanted a suspicious gaze at her. "I can't believe that you've finally accepted the validity of my research."

"Not quite."

And with the ungallant way he was behaving, she certainly wasn't going to admit that she was looking forward to being alone with him on the open plains. To the time they would spend together. To the next occasion when he took her in his arms.

"Then what? Why aren't you complaining and telling me I'm crazy?"

"I don't know." She shrugged. "Blame it on Dawn Fire."

He gestured to the saddlebags. "You're going to need some kind of magic to pack all your junk into those bags."

Hands on hips, she looked from the mountain of purchases to the skimpy space he expected her to use. It didn't take an Einstein to deduce that the mass of her supplies wouldn't fit into the existing space he offered. "I'll need another two bags, at least."

"Not a chance." He went to sit on her soft bed, then thought better of it and planted himself on the low-backed but heavy rocking chair beside the window. "No more space. We're taking three horses. One that's strictly a pack animal, and that horse is going to be loaded with food and cooking utensils. We'll have two other horses for riding and carrying some light supplies."

"But really, McCloud—"

"This is all the space you have. We're an archaeological expedition, not a traveling circus."

In her mind, Sandra phrased an argument, but she recognized the cool glint in his turquoise eyes and decided against trying to change his mind. While she'd been shopping in Santa Fe, Sandra had been in control. Now it was McCloud's turn. It was his expedition, and he wanted her to know that he was the boss. She fired off a salute. "Yessir, no more bags."

"I'm glad you understand."

"Indeed. You're the fearless leader, after all. And I'm only the... What am I, anyway?"

"Damned if I know."

"If you don't know my job for this trek, why am I coming along?"

"Because I trust Martin White Horse, and he seems to think that you've got some kind of luck or intuition that will lead me to the city of gold."

"What?" She didn't like the sound of that. Not in the least. Her feminist principles were outraged. Back in Denver, she'd thought McCloud was using Martin White Horse to get her back to his ranch, so she hadn't given Martin's words much credence. "Excuse me, McCloud, but are you saying that I'm some kind of lucky charm?"

"But much prettier than a rabbit's foot or a horseshoe."

He was a jerk, after all. McCloud was nothing more than a sexist jerk. And so was Martin White Horse. And Jessop. And Max the Ax, back in Denver. He had to be snickering every time he thought of Sandra being dragged through the wilds of southern Colorado on a quest for a mythical city of gold. It would serve them all right if she found this El Dorado.

She kicked at her purchases. "I can fit them in. And I guarantee that you're going to thank me for some of the things I'm bringing along."

"I already want to thank you for the fine coffee you brought back from Santa Fe."

She'd arranged with a specialty store to have fresh coffee mailed to the ranch every week for the next month. After that, she figured McCloud and the cowboys would be so attached to the special Colombian blend that they'd be willing to chip in the extra couple of bucks for the good beans. Elena had agreed, both with her logic and with the taste of the coffee.

"You're welcome," Sandra said.

He tipped back in the rocker. "I can't wait to see how you're going to pack that junk."

"Obviously, I can't take it all. Some things have to be eliminated."

"Like the hair dryer? And the fancy coffee-maker?"

"Those are necessities. Besides, I can use the blow dryer to dry other things. Like my clothes if it rains."

"Or if you fall in a creek?"

"I doubt that will happen, but if it does, this time I'm prepared." She whirled on him, aimed her blow dryer and fired a blast of hot air. Her eyes narrowed as she glared at him. "How about guns? If those renegades are out there, I want to be armed."

"I'll carry the guns."

"That is so sexist, McCloud." She stamped her foot for emphasis. "I know how to use a rifle. My father taught me when he was going through his Hemingway period. And I'm passable with a handgun."

"Okay, here's the deal. Even though it's unlikely that we'll need firearms, except for defending ourselves against vicious sagebrush, I'll take along two rifles and two handguns. While we're camping, I'll show you how to use these particular models."

"Fair enough."

She stared back at the heap on the floor, hoping that it had somehow compacted itself into a manageable stack. But the pile was still there.

"How about leaving out your clothes?" he suggested. "You don't really need anything more than that thermal underwear."

"You'd like that, wouldn't you?"

He gave a comical leer. "You'd look real cute, riding into the sunset wearing nothing but that fancy union suit that fits like a second skin. Your little bottom would be bouncing up and down in the saddle."

"Let's keep my rear end out of this discussion."

"But that's exactly what I want to talk about. Your bottom. Your long legs. Your smooth, creamy white—"

"Forget it, McCloud. I have to pack."

He joined her on the floor. "I'll help."

The first item he picked from her stack was a lacy black bra. The filmy fabric tangled sexily in his fingers like a spider's web. He was almost blushing when he untangled himself. But he said, "Definitely take this."

"My bra? Of course, I'm taking that."

She snatched it away from him. Tonight was so different from last night's intense sensuality. He seemed to be joking, hiding his feelings behind the facade of a teasing cowboy who was baffled by a lady's undergarment. Sandra would lay money on the odds that he'd removed enough bras in his day to be an expert.

The physical attraction was still there, still powerful as a force of nature. But there was confusion. When they weren't in bed together, their roles lacked definition. Sandra had never fit the standard stereotype of a woman in a relationship. Maybe she was too competitive. Maybe she didn't have time for all the give and take.

Or, in this case, giving in. For a moment, she regretted the ease with which he'd swept her off her feet. Her resistance to him had been pathetically nonexistent, which was so unlike her. Though she'd never seen the point in playing hard to get, Sandra was cautious in her choice of mates and didn't flit from man to man. McCloud was the first man she'd been intimate with in over three years. And it had been much longer since she'd imagined herself to be in love.

Love. She sighed. Neither one of them dared even mention the word. At dinner, McCloud had sipped the freshly brewed coffee and said that he "liked it a lot." She'd sat on the porch with him and mentioned how she "enjoyed" the sunset. *Love* was expunged from their vocabularies.

Which was just as well, she thought. Because after love came words like *commitment* and *sharing* and all sorts of other difficult vocabulary that was better left unsaid.

She glanced up from her stack of clothes and met his gaze. Before he could look away, she saw a glimmer of last night's passion in his eyes. He was wearing a blue shirt and the turquoise was even brighter than usual.

Ignoring the little flutter in her heart, she attacked the pile. No matter how tightly she packed the clothes, it wouldn't all fit. Something had to go. With a sigh, she eliminated the hair dryer. And the third pair of shoes. She pared her clothing to the bare essentials, but it still wasn't enough. Her packing was coming down to a choice between the coffeemaker and the air mattress.

Should she pamper her backside or her taste buds? "All right, I hate to do this. But I'll leave out the coffeemaker. I'll give it to Elena."

"You seem real concerned about that woman's caffeine intake."

"I'm concerned that she's being browbeaten by all you men and not appreciated."

"Elena? She runs that kitchen like a major general." More seriously, he added, "She's good at her work, and she's well paid, Sandra. Even out here on the ranch, we're socially conscious enough not to treat Elena like a kitchen slave."

"I wasn't implying that."

"Sure you were. You were about to get all righteous because Elena is the only female around here and she does traditional woman's work in the kitchen. You've got to remember, Sandra. Housekeeping is Elena's career."

Properly chastised, Sandra said, "This is the second time today that I've forgotten that women who aren't doctors or accountants or lawyers can also be career women."

"The second time?"

"My mother," she said, tucking her lightweight sneakers into the corner of the saddlebag. "When I saw the work of her student being accepted and sold, it occurred to me that my mother had a career. Even though she was paid for her paintings and paid by students, I never thought of her as a professional person. Art was just something that Emma did."

She fastened the strap on the last saddlebag. "Hah! I'm done."

"About time."

This time, when she caught his gaze, McCloud didn't look away. His eyes held an intensity that made her nervous and excited at the same time. Without saying a single word, he made it clear that the invitation was there. If she wanted to make love tonight, he would be more than happy to comply.

And then what? Though her body yearned for him, she knew that lovemaking was a prelude to losing control. Sandra wasn't sure that would be a wise choice. She rose to her feet, stretched and yawned. "We leave at dawn tomorrow?"

"That's right."

But what about tonight? The unspoken question dangled between them.

If Sandra was completely honest with herself, she would invite him into her bed. They would make love, give each other that rare special pleasure. But she wasn't sure if she should. If they made love tonight, they would surely make love tomorrow. And they were scheduled for six days of searching before they returned to the ranch. Their time together might be as idyllic as a honeymoon. Or it could be disastrous.

She couldn't decide whether it was less insulting to be taken on this search as a lucky charm or as a sex object. Neither was what she wanted to be. "We should talk about some ground rules, McCloud."

"Ground rules?"

"For the time that we're going to be spending together."

"Are you talking about a contract, Sandra?"

She pounced happily at that familiar concept. Contracts were something she could deal with. "Exactly. A contract that details what I can expect from you, and vice versa."

He stepped up beside her. "I'll take care of the horses."

Though division of chores wasn't what she had in mind, Sandra was willing to start there. "And I'll make coffee in the morning. Since I'm a morning person, I'll probably be awake first anyway."

"We'll share the cooking." He touched her cheek, tucked her hair behind her ear. "And the cleanup."

She caught his hand, suppressing the tremor that shot through her the moment their flesh made contact. Her voice was earnest. "Actually, McCloud, this is more what I was talking about. The potential for touching and kissing and other things."

He chuckled. "You want a contract about sex?"

"I think it might be appropriate. We're a man and a woman who will, by necessity, be alone for a fairly lengthy period of time. Even Max insinuated that there might be a problem."

"Max?"

"A jerk who works at the law firm."

"I see. And do you always discuss your personal life with your associates?"

"Only when it's applicable to business. And this quest? It's business."

Without warning, he grasped her waist and pulled her close to him. "How about this, Sandra? Is hugging all right?"

She gasped.

"A little hug," he said. "Surely you can't object to that?"

The length of his body molded against hers could hardly be called a hug. They were thigh to thigh. Her breasts crushed against his hard chest. Being this close to him was a highly erotic experience. And yet she said, "I suppose an occasional hug would be acceptable behavior."

"How occasional?"

"I don't know." Her senses began to reel. She had to put some air space between them before she turned into a blithering mass of desire.

He pressed the question. "Once or twice a day?"

"Yes," she said formally. "A hug once or twice a day."

His mouth claimed hers for a fierce kiss that bruised her lips and quickened her pulse. She fought the urges that coursed along her veins.

Abruptly he pulled away. "And kissing. Is kissing acceptable?"

"Damn it, McCloud."

"Can I take that as a yes?"

"No." Her eyes sought his face. Her parted lips trembled, longing for another kiss while denying it at the same time. "No kissing."

"Not even when it's like this?"

With deliberate thoroughness, he tasted her mouth again. His tongue thrust deep, caressing her, cajoling her. And she responded, savoring the slick surface of his teeth.

When he released her, Sandra was woozy. Weakly she said, "I told you no."

"That didn't feel like a no."

"I can't trust you, McCloud. I'm trying to make a contract and you're—"

"Can't trust me? Let's not go through this again." He moved away from her. His smoldering passion turned to anger. "You damn well trusted me enough to go to bed with me."

His words stung, but only because the truth was painful. She had given him her body, shared the most private part of herself. Talking about trust, about having to earn her trust, could have been ridiculous. But she still had her pride. "I won't be manipulated, McCloud."

"You're right about that, lady." He opened the door. "We leave at dawn. Be ready."

She stared at the door as he pulled it shut. What had happened here? In a matter of moments, she'd gone from being fondly caressed to being soundly rejected. Or had she rejected him?

Either way, it didn't feel right. And she wasn't looking forward to six days and five nights of the same.

AS DAWN'S FIRE STREAKED the skies, they made ready to depart. Sandra shook Pablo's hand and embraced Letty and Elena.

McCloud avoided any contact with her. Barely speaking to her, he'd mounted up and was waiting, staring into the magenta-and-gold skies with that faraway look that was peculiar to men who worked outdoors.

She swung onto the wide back of the dappled mare named Sugar and said to McCloud, "I'm ready. Let's go."

It would have been dramatic to canter past the barn and into the open prairie. The "William Tell Overture" would have made for a stirring exit. But this was a calm archaeological expedition. At a slow rolling, side-to-side pace, the horses plodded through the yard.

She waved goodbye to her friends and to the ranch house that had come to mean something special to her—something that almost felt like home.

Sandra should have been excited to set out. Challenges always excited her. But she was tense. "McCloud, do you have a good feeling about this expedition?"

"I always do. Every time I begin a new search, I think this is it. This is the time when I'm going to find something. But I never do. All I've found, in eight years, is a sack full of pot shards and arrowheads."

They rode silently for several minutes, then Sandra remembered. "I forgot to tell Letty where to find my car keys. She needed to use my car when she got back to Denver."

"Too bad, we're on our way and we're not going back."

"No problem." From the saddlebag on her horse, she pulled out the cellular phone and punched out the number for the ranch. It rang three times before Pablo answered, and Sandra gave him the message about her keys in case Letty needed her car while she was gone.

After she hung up, she tossed a smug grin to McCloud. "Wasn't that convenient? I took care of my business and we didn't miss a stride. And just think how useful this phone will be if, God forbid, one of us is hurt or sick."

"Just don't leave it where I can reach it. I can barely put up with having phones in my office, and I hate taking one out here."

"Why? What if you needed help?" Teasing, she continued, "Is this one of those macho things where you'd rather drag yourself for hundreds of miles with a broken leg than ask for help?"

"I can ask for help," he said defensively. "On occasion, I've even been known to ask for directions."

"Then why do you hate telephone technology?"

"There's no cord, but it feels like there is. It's intrusive." The wind had picked up. As they rode through a vast desert valley, small twirling dust devils popped up on either side of them. "I don't know, Sandra. There's a time and place for technology. Out here, I want the land kept pure, almost sacred."

"So? People take beepers into church all the time." His distaste was so evident, she couldn't help adding, "How else is God going to reach the Yuppies?"

He laughed, and Sandra felt an easing of the tightness that stretched between them. Maybe this expedition wouldn't be so wretched, after all. If they could relate on a level of friendship... "McCloud, after everything that has happened between us, do you think we could be friends?"

The brim of his hat shaded his eyes, making it difficult for her to read his expression. "We are," he said, adding, "real unlikely friends."

"Why?"

"What do we have in common? Outside the bedroom, I mean?"

She winced. "That's a frank assessment."

"I don't tiptoe around with friends. That's part of it. I've got to be able to say what I'm thinking. Without worrying that I might hurt your feelings."

This might be more difficult than she thought. Sandra had very few male friends. In fact, there were none who weren't somehow professional associates. "Okay, McCloud, sure. I might not be able to do male bonding, but I can be frank. Tell me what you're thinking."

"I want you to trust me, Sandra."

"You really slice right to the heart of things, don't you?" Her distrust was based on so many things. "This is going to take time. But I guess we've got lots of that."

They hadn't seen another soul, not another mammal, since they'd left the ranch. Overhead, the golden sunrise had burned away and the blue of the sky deepened in hue. Perfect solitude surrounded them.

"Time," he said, "is one thing we have plenty of. How long is it going to take for you to trust me?"

An idea struck her and she turned in the saddle. "I know how I can do this. I'll presume that you are innocent. Instead of starting with the assumption that you're a scam artist who bilked my parents and tied up my own cash from their investment ... Instead of believing that you somehow conned Martin White Horse into using his influence at my law firm ..."

"Damn, Sandra, you have a way with words. The way you phrased that makes me feel all warm inside."

She ignored his sarcasm. "Bear with me, McCloud. This could work. Once I had a client who looked totally guilty, but somehow I knew, I just knew he wasn't."

"A murderer?"

"Nothing so dramatic. It was a white-collar crime. He was accused of fraud and embezzlement, and the facts pointed right straight at him. But I knew Stuart wasn't guilty. There wasn't any reason for me to believe it, but I was certain. So I looked at everything from his angle—Stuart's angle—until I found proof. He was innocent as a newborn baby."

"Why are you making this so hard? If you want to trust me, go head and trust me. Emotional decisions aren't always logical."

She started to say that she never ever made emotional decisions, but stopped herself. Making love with him had not been logical. But it had felt right. And good. And truthful. "If I start making decisions about what feels good, nothing makes sense."

Because she didn't feel good about being ordered to come down here by Mr. Jessop. She definitely didn't feel good about the presumption that she'd do whatever was required for the firm without consideration for her own ethics.

And, if she carried that thinking to the bitter end, it probably meant she didn't feel good about being a partner. Yet how could she give that up? She'd worked so hard to achieve the status of partner. She couldn't throw it away because it didn't *feel* right, didn't *feel* truthful, but how could she pursue ambitions that were full of compromise and lies?

"Sandra?"

"Sorry, I was thinking about something else."

He peered down to look in her face. "Must have been a good thought. You've got that determined little smirk that means nobody is going to stop you. Nohow. No way."

"I just realized that I might have to give up my partnership at Jessop, Feldner and White."

She clicked her heels against the flanks of her dappled mare and rode a little farther. Not galloping, but pulling away from him.

McCloud shook his head as he watched her shoulders bouncing ahead of him. He would never understand this female. For such a smart person, she made the most bizarre leaps in logic he had ever seen. Give up her partnership?

He remembered the first time he'd seen her, pristine in white and brimming with the pleasure of her big accomplishment. And now she was willing to give it up because she'd made some mental connection while riding through the dusty desert on a search for the city of gold.

Riding up beside her, he dragged her back to the subject at hand. "Okay, Sandra. I'll play your game. This will be our courtroom. So if you assume I'm innocent..."

"Not an assumption. It's a knowing." She tapped her breast. "Here, deep inside me, I know that you really are trustworthy no matter how the facts appear."

"So what happens next?"

"I depose you. Now, this isn't a cross-examination, because I'm not trying to prove you wrong. But I'm playing devil's advocate. So don't get insulted. Okay?"

"Shoot."

"First, we'll talk about Martin White Horse, and the reason I had to come back to the ranch."

They rehashed the whole scenario. Bottom line, Sandra discovered, was hearsay. McCloud claimed he didn't know Martin would go to Jessop and request Sandra's presence on the quest.

"But I think Martin's motives were pure," McCloud said. "For some reason, he's got it in his head that you are the key to finding this city of gold."

"In other words," Sandra clarified, "you didn't tell him that you had the hots for me and you'd appreciate the favor of getting me down here."

"The hots for you?" McCloud chuckled. "I'm not a teenager."

"But you are a man."

"And what's that supposed to mean?"

"You do things like wear Levi's for four days in a row. And you're aggressive about sexual attraction. Since you're not the type to sweet-talk me or send me flowers..."

"What type am I?"

"You're a cowboy. No, you're a prospector. But there's the Native American side to you." She shrugged. "You're the type to see what you want and go after it. If I hadn't come down here on my own, I wouldn't have been surprised to find you waiting outside my downtown Denver office on horseback. You'd grab me up, throw me over your saddle and carry me off into the sunset."

"And you'd like that, wouldn't you?"

Primly she responded, "I admit I like a man who knows his mind, but I would hate being carried off forcefully. If you tried to abduct me, I would probably sue your cowboy/prospector/Indian butt for assault."

They went around the question of Martin White Horse again, still coming back to McCloud's assertion that he hadn't had contact with the old Navajo man since he'd seen him at the campfire. There were no facts to the contrary.

"So you say." Sandra frowned. "But you can't prove it."

"I suppose there's no telephone record of me calling him. That's proof. And there's no witness to me and Martin talking."

"Circumstantial." She gestured to the open prairie. "There aren't an abundance of witnesses."

They stopped for lunch beside a creek and devoured the sandwiches and apples that Elena had packed that morning. While they ate, Sandra turned the problem of Martin White Horse over and over in her mind. There was no proof. None. "Unless I talk to Martin," she said between bites. "Even then, you and he might have arranged for him to lie to me."

"Martin White Horse?" McCloud took a long sip of cool water. "Come on, Sandra. You couldn't find a more venerable person. He's an elder in the Navajo tribe. White-haired. Wise in the ways of spirits and of men."

Cynically she asked, "Does that mean he never lies?"

"Never. People like Martin are practically part of the earth, no more capable of lying than the water in this creek is capable of stopping its flow."

Sandra sat back to consider the implications. If Martin White Horse, the canny old Navajo who dealt with Denver lawyers, truly believed the story he'd told Laurence Jessop, then she was, in some weird way, connected to the myths and legends.

If Martin was correct, she was a lucky charm, a reincarnation of Dawn Fire. If that was true, Sandra reasoned, the discovery of the golden city rested in her hands.

A shiver went through her.

Strange and illogical as those assumptions seemed, they felt right and true.

Chapter Eleven

The first canyon they searched in the afternoon turned up no clues. Though Sandra discovered a nest of pheasants in the mesquite and startled a whole family of jackrabbits that bounded away with athletic leaps that would put Michael Jordan to shame, the walls and floor of the narrow canyon were unremarkable.

They reached a small box canyon, and McCloud dismounted in a small circular clearing. After digging around with his toe, he knelt and felt in the soil with his fingertips.

Though she watched him carefully, trying to learn something about this strange land, her gaze focused on his broad shoulders and the taut pull of denim across his thighs. She had to drag her attention away from him and force herself not to think about nightfall and sleeping arrangements.

When he stood, he held out his hand and showed her three hard stones, roughly chiseled. Arrowheads.

She wouldn't have been more astounded if he'd pulled a rabbit out of his cowboy hat. "How did you find those?"

He turned the arrowheads in his hand and explained, "Because the vegetation is so sparse, this land bears the imprint of almost everything that's happened to it. In some places, you can still see the parallel mark of wheels from the covered wagons. A trail that was made a hundred and fifty years ago."

She nodded, fascinated. "What made you think there were arrowheads here?"

"This little circle clearing didn't seem natural to me. It looked like someone stopped here and cleared away a space for camping and spending the night. That someone might have been a Boy Scout. Or a warrior." He studied the shape of the arrowhead. "From the Ute tribe."

"Why wasn't it buried under layers and layers of dirt?"

"Sometimes they are. But the topsoil here is minimal unless the land has been fertilized and irrigated. Sometimes, things are buried for years and years, then the rains come and wash away the dirt, leaving artifacts exposed."

The possibility of actually finding something of importance became more probable in her eyes. "McCloud? What are you doing?"

He tossed the arrowheads back to the earth. "I'm leaving these here. I have dozens of them."

"But why?"

"Once, a long time ago, I'd picked up almost enough shards to form a complete pot. Then I dreamed that the woman who had used that bowl came through a spiritual mist to seek the object she'd fashioned with her own hands. It didn't seem right to remove it, to leave her spirit wandering restlessly."

"You're superstitious," she said. "That sounds like being haunted by a ghost."

"Or haunted by my native heritage. My grand-mother always told me to treat the land with respect, to thank the earth for its bounty and to never take more than I need."

"Good philosophy."

As she turned and headed back toward her mount, Sugar, he caught her hand. She pivoted quickly and faced him. "What is it, McCloud?"

"You agreed with me, Sandra. We have something in common."

He released his grasp and went to his horse, leaving her with a sense of surprise and bewilderment. Something in common?

But not really, she thought.

Of course, she agreed with the importance of conservation. It was vital not to take more from the environment than was needed and to replenish the harvest. But Sandra's life-style did not reflect such high-minded thoughts. She had plans to purchase a condo and a better car. She swam in a chlorinated pool. She paid lip service while McCloud actually lived by these admirable concerns. Hard to believe, from a man she didn't trust.

That night they camped in a sheltered area not far from a creek. The landscape was desolate, similar to the first canyon where she'd found McCloud, and Sandra couldn't help making comparisons. There was the obvious difference: Sandra was not wet. And the subtle difference: she was not angry.

Also, since she had taken time to prepare for this journey, she was comfortable in her flexible soled boots and warm in her thermal jacket. A pleasant sense of well-being surrounded her as she leaned back against a rock and faced the west to watch the sun slide behind the San Juans.

McCloud noticed her change in attitude as he came up and sat beside her. "You've come a long way, baby."

"Yes, I have." The fading sunset colored the sky a subtle tapestry. The rustling of the creek and whistling wind were a symphony. "It's beautiful."

"Nothing better. Nature is the master, and everything else is just imitation."

"And the sun. You keep talking about the earth as the source, but it's really the sun." She picked up a stick and doodled in the gravelly earth. "I think there are as many sun god legends as earth mother. In almost all the tribes."

"Especially with the Aztecs."

She nodded. "A blood sacrifice every day. And they believed that if they missed, even once, the sun would not come up."

"A fascinating culture. Completely wiped out."

"Hey, you were the one who told me that cultures are never extinct. Parts of them are absorbed into others." She'd drawn a stick figure and put sun rays around the head. "It seems to me that the Aztecs really are the most likely beginning for your city of gold legends."

"Aztecs? In Colorado?"

It was extremely unlikely that the people of Montezuma, who were really a more urban population, had ventured into this cold and rugged land. And yet, Sandra sensed there was a connection between McCloud's quest and the extravagant sun worship of the ancient Aztecs.

There was the coincidence of the maiden's name—always a celestial reference. She was persistently portrayed as a sun goddess. And, of course, the symbolism of gold and the sun was unmistakable.

Sandra explained her thoughts to McCloud, and he nodded. "Could be that you're on to something. I had always believed that the people of legend were a Plains tribe. Nomadic and wandering until Dawn Fire led them to the place where they would settle down, take root and flourish."

"Exactly what are we searching for?" she asked. "I know this isn't a literal city of gold, but is it something like Mesa Verde?"

"I imagine so."

"I hate to say this, McCloud, but maybe your fabled city has already been found. Mesa Verde could be the place. It's huge. Very complex. There are kivas and storage bins, terraced gardens on the surrounding lands. How will your city be different?"

"It will be golden." He had always imagined the city of Dawn Fire and her warrior to be a sacred site, a mystical place. His dreams told him that it had not been found. "When I see the city of gold, in my mind, it's almost perfect. Though no one has been there for hundreds of years, there is no dust on the tables and chairs. And there is gold, precious metals that have been fashioned into bowls and masks. There are answers there to the archaeological question of what happened to the Anasazi, why these civilizations existed and why they seemed to vanish."

"Sounds flaky, McCloud."

"A little," he agreed. "What's even stranger is that I won't be disappointed if I never find the city. Part of the reward is the dream itself."

"A quest for enlightenment?"

She cocked her head to one side and studied his handsome profile. This man was a buffalo rancher in southern Colorado, not a knight errant seeking the Holy Grail. And yet, she imagined, there were similarities. The same strange fever burned within all seekers, lighting their paths and driving them to search.

Illogical as his quest might be, she found him admirable. Not many people had the guts to believe in possibilities beyond everyday life, much less to pursue their dreams.

At that moment, with the sweet-smelling dusk closing around them, she found McCloud more attractive than ever before. But not in a sensual way. His spirit called to hers, and she was drawn to answer.

Almost as if he sensed her mood, he turned toward her. His hand grasped the firm muscles of her knee and gave a friendly squeeze. "You understand what I'm saying, don't you?"

"I'm not sure yet." She took his hand and removed it. "And until I am, not even a hug is permissible."

"No problem." He held up both hands where she could see them. "Anticipation is half the fun."

"There's no guarantee that we'll make love again, McCloud. We might be incompatible."

The last rays of sunlight burnished his clean-shaven cheek. "No, Sandra, that's not possible."

The warmth of his gaze and the nearness of his body were a powerful temptation, but she scooted away from him, putting a safety cushion of several inches between them. "What's the plan for our search?"

"I have it all mapped out. I should have gone over that with you while it was still light. But now . . . well, it's better if we don't get into the habit of having a fire."

"Tell you what, McCloud, it's about time for you to enter the twentieth century." She rose to her feet and dusted off her bottom. "Won't you join me in my tent?"

"We can't have a bright light in there, either. The silly thing will glow like a beacon."

"Not so. Didn't you listen when I was talking to the clerk?" She led him to her tent. The fabric was black, opaque and it was almost invisible in the night.

The tent popped up to a height of nearly six feet and the base was a six foot square. She opened the flap and ducked inside. "Go get your maps, then come back here."

Inside the tent, she turned on a small battery-powered lamp that threw off a great deal of light in a small area. The clerk at the sporting goods store promised that the light inside the tent would be invisible from the outside, and she was sure McCloud would tell her if that assumption was incorrect.

He stumbled at the tent door. His voice was surprised when he opened the flap. "You've got a light in here."

"Correct. And you couldn't see it from outside?"

"Not at all." He sat cross-legged on the sleeping bag she'd spread over the pumped-up air mattress. "Very cozy."

"It's all a matter of being prepared." Her grin was smug. "Too bad that you'll be sleeping outside on the cold hard ground."

"Really too bad."

"Such a shame! But you wouldn't listen to me, thought I was being a silly female, didn't believe that camping doesn't have to be a hardship."

He spread out the maps between them. Under his breath, he muttered, "Okay, you were right."

"I didn't quite hear that."

"Good job, Sandra."

The map he had was a copy of the aerial photograph in his office, but half as big. Several areas were blacked out. He pointed to a place that looked like a hand spread out flat. The fingers were canyons. "This is where we are."

"And where did we see that guy with the gun?"

He traced a line all the way across the map to the eastern edge of the search area. Almost all the canyons were blacked out. He indicated one of the larger spaces. "Right about here."

"But we have no need to go back to their hideout, right?"

"It's not a hideout. These guys aren't the hole-in-the-wall gang. They were probably only stopping there for the night."

"And then?"

He shrugged. "Pablo thinks they're rustlers. They might be running drugs from Mexico. Or guns."

She shuddered, hating to think of how helpless they were in the desert. Reaching into her bag, she took out the cellular phone. "How would I describe our position to the sheriff?"

"Sandra, by the time the sheriff got here, it would be too late." With obvious disgust, he took the phone from her hand. "Tomorrow, first thing, I'll give you a gun. But I really don't think you'll need it."

"Why not? If those renegades or rustlers or whatever they are come snooping around here—"

"They'll be delighted by all this expensive stuff. They probably won't even notice us. This loot is the jackpot."

She sank back into her own thoughts, a confusing miasma of worry and wondering. Everything about this journey held an element of danger. And yet she felt safe. Then there was the constant emotional hazard of being so physically close to McCloud...and the desire to be closer.

When he headed toward the tent flap, she said, "Wait! You can stay in here. No hugging, no touching, no kissing. But there's no need for you to be outside."

"Yes, there is." He looked back at her. "I'm trying to prove myself trustworthy. If I sleep in here, it's doubtful that I'll make it through the night without wanting to touch you, Sandra. I won't be able to sleep when I'm this close to you, able to smell the fragrance of your hair, to hear the little catch in your breathing when you sleep."

"Snoring? I don't snore."

"And I don't have that much self-control. Staying outside is better," he continued as he unzipped the flap. "Almost as good as a cold shower."

And then he was gone, vanished into the blackness beyond her tent. "Good night, McCloud," she whispered.

He had left the map behind, and she stretched out on her sleeping bag to stare at the strange foreshortened picture. It took some careful study to discern a three-dimensional perspective from the flattened photograph. And the size was difficult to determine because of the shadows. Depending upon the angle, some trees looked as big as mountains.

She changed into her thermal underwear and snuggled into the sleeping bag, then studied the map again. They seemed to be moving in a northern search pattern, and she figured that since they'd only managed to go through two canyons this afternoon, they might be spending a whole week in these outstretched fingers. What if it was the wrong place? They would have wasted a week, and there wasn't much time left. Only a few more days and then . . .

She turned off the light, lay still and listened. Outside her tent, McCloud was setting up his own sleeping bag. Though he was silent on his moccasined feet, she heard small rustlings and her imagination went wild. Taking off his Levi's? Slipping out of his shirt? She guessed a guy like McCloud could withstand the cold. . . .

She thought of his bare chest, broad and magnificent, covered with thick, dark hair. Her last thought before sleeping was a vision of his turquoise eyes, looking at her with an unmistakable expression of desire that she longed to fulfill.

THE NEXT MORNING, after a quick breakfast and packing up, McCloud passed her a rifle. His expression was doubtful. "You're sure you've handled guns before."

In reply, Sandra loaded, cocked, positioned the barrel, looked down the sight and fired. The branch on a cottonwood tree flicked up and down. She set the rifle down. "It pulls to the left."

"You're right." He laughed. "Is there anything you don't do well?"

Relationships, she thought. Sandra didn't do at all well with relationships. But that wasn't the sort of information she wanted to share. "Can I carry the rifle?"

"Now that I know you won't accidentally shoot off your toes? Sure."

He helped her fasten the holster to her saddle, and they started out again. It was slightly warmer than the day before, and Sandra stripped down to her cotton shirt by lunchtime. She rolled the sleeves all the way up to her shoulders. At McCloud's puzzled look, she explained, "Tan line."

In the late morning, Sandra decided to walk for a ways. Her rear and thighs were beginning to ache from the full day of riding, and McCloud strode along beside her. His eyes were always busy, scanning the walls of the cliffs and searching for signs on the ground.

"McCloud, I want to talk about this trust thing."

"What about it?"

"I want to know the real, honest-to-goodness reason you came to Denver and searched me out at the Athletic Club."

"I came to Denver for *Cinco de Mayo*," he said with a sigh. "That is a provable fact. I've only missed one celebration in the past twelve years. You can check with Elena. Or Pablo. Or anybody who knows me well."

"Why? I mean, I know it's a special day for a lot of people. But why for you?"

"My Ute grandmother died on the fifth of May, and she's buried in a cemetery in Denver." He stooped to pick up a stone, and pitched it hard, nicking the edge of a juniper branch. "It was a good death . . . if there is such a thing. She was very old. She'd been ill, had pneumonia and we took her to a hospital in Denver. She was only there for a day when she died in her sleep with a smile on her face."

He still remembered the pain. And the fury. An explosion of rage inside his gut had threatened to tear him apart. Though his grandmother had told him that it was her time to go and she was glad, McCloud had been furious.

"I was angry. At her," he said. "Does that seem wrong?"

"Seems perfectly natural to me."

He picked another smooth stone from the ground, threw it high in the air and caught it. "I've never told anyone that before. About the anger."

She felt glad that he could trust her. Desperately, she wished she could reciprocate that trust. "Then what happened?"

"I went out into the streets. There were all those bright colors and music. I wasn't even ten years old, but a pretty girl grabbed my arm and pulled me into the crowd, and I spent the rest of the day and well into the night dancing. Then, I guess, I was too tired to be angry anymore."

He shrugged. "Now I go back to Denver every year on the fifth of May. I try to celebrate my grandmother's life. Not her death. Standing at her grave, every year, is a way of taking stock of my life."

She knew exactly what he meant. Birthdays were the benchmark she used to gauge her progress. Though other people might look at her life and be amazed at the progress, Sandra was never satisfied.

"I came to see you," he said, "because I happened to be in town, and your parents had told me a lot about you."

"Not because you wanted to soften me up before my parents told me about the investment?"

"The thought might have crossed my mind," he admitted. "I might have figured that an attorney would give me a hard time about my contracts. But I have my own lawyer to handle those things."

"Why didn't you refer me to him? The very first time, when I called, why didn't you give me his name?"

"I wanted to see you again."

If that wasn't manipulative behavior, she didn't know what was. And yet it was a compliment. "McCloud, if you wanted to see me again, why didn't you just say so? When I called you, the first time, why didn't you tell me that you wanted me to come to Alamosa?"

With a teasing grin, he said, "I'm shy?"

"Shy as a blue-eyed hawk."

He halted in his tracks and stared at her. "Now you're the one who's not telling everything."

"What?"

"You've been talking to Martin White Horse."

"I haven't seen that sneaky old gentleman since he showed up at Jessop, Feldner and White. McCloud, what's wrong? Why are you looking at me like that?"

"Nothing." He looked up in the noon sky. "We'll stop here for lunch."

He busied himself with taking care of the horses while Sandra took care of the food preparations. A couple of times she caught him eyeing her suspiciously. When they sat down, she demanded an explanation.

He answered her with a question. "How do you feel about the legend?"

"It's interesting. Folk tales are always interesting."

"You're here," he said, "not because I manipulated you, but because of Martin White Horse. There's something in you that he likes. And, Sandra, you don't know how unusual that is. Martin isn't a kindly guy. He comes from warrior stock."

"Warrior stock?" There was a time when she would have scoffed at such a statement. But no more. "Could you explain what that means?"

"Martin isn't so much a spiritual man as he is a strong leader. Damn strong physically. Once, in a bar, I saw him arm wrestle a man half his age to his knees."

"What does that have to do with me?"

"Martin doesn't usually pay much attention to white men, and he totally disregards white women. But he went to a hell of a lot of trouble to get you down here."

"So?"

"What if there really is something to this legend? What if there's some kind of weird connection that reached through time and space to arrange for you and me to be together at this moment in this place?"

A shiver went through her. She sensed the presence of unseen eyes. "I don't believe in that stuff, McCloud."

He took both her hands in his. "The way you've been with me. That's not the way you've been with any other man."

"Not usually."

"Not ever."

He was right. She had never made love to a man she'd only known for a few hours. And the passion he aroused in her exceeded anything else she'd ever known. "What's your point, McCloud?"

"You've dropped enough odd little phrases that I have a hard time remembering that you're a big-city attorney. And how many other attorneys know how to shoot and ride?"

"Several, I'm sure. Attorneys aren't born with law books in their hands."

"There's something else going on here. You spoke of a blue-eyed hawk."

"So?"

"Blue Hawk. It's my Indian name. Martin uses it. The only other person who spoke that name was my grandmother."

"It's a coincidence, McCloud."

"Maybe." He squeezed her hands and dropped them. "But maybe, Sandra, we're part of a larger destiny. You might know secrets that you are unaware of knowing."

They finished eating before McCloud picked up this line of thinking again. "This afternoon I want you to go over the map. See if there's any area that speaks to you."

"Speaks to me?" she asked skeptically.

"Just try it, okay? I'll search the next canyon alone while you stay here and think."

"Meditate?" What new age nonsense! Sandra had experienced quite enough of that sort of thinking while she was growing up and her parents had guru-like friends who played with crystals and burned incense.

Still, she didn't mind spending the afternoon resting instead of riding and walking. "Okay, McCloud. I'll keep the rifle with me in case I'm visited by someone other than the great spirit."

After he left, she dug out a pair of shorts and a tank top from her saddlebag. The sun was warm enough for tanning, and Sandra arranged her body on a rock with the aerial map spread out in front of her. She wasn't sleepy, but a pleasant lassitude spread over her, a contentment. The sun was warm, but there was just enough breeze to keep her from sweating.

She looked up. In the distance, the plateaus and mesas seemed blue. The shadows of fluffy cumulus clouds moved ponderously across the land.

Staring down at the map, she waited for some sort of mystical pull. But she felt nothing. Remembering how McCloud had been able to locate the arrowheads, she looked for patterns. But, of course, that was ridiculous. These photos had been taken from hundreds of feet overhead. Small signs would not be evident. Then a darkness fell across the map—the shadow of a man.

Instantly, Sandra sprang to her feet. Martin White Horse stood beside her, blocking the sun. His long white hair, free from the bun he usually wore, blew around her shoulders. His expression was stern.

"How are you, Sandra?"

"Where did you come from?"

"This is my land."

Sandra wasn't sure whether she was asleep or awake. There was a dreamlike quality to Martin and his low calm voice. "There's something I have to know," she said. "When you came to the law firm, had you talked to McCloud first?"

"I did not need to consult McCloud. When I saw you, I knew. A woman must lead him. I knew you were the woman."

"Dawn Fire?"

"But first, there must be trust between you. The trust of one mate for another."

"A mate?" She gathered her wits around her. "Listen, Martin, your culture has many fascinating beliefs and legends, but there's no way you could know that McCloud and I should mate."

He stood silently.

"I mean, really, Martin. Haven't you heard of compatibility? And shared interests? Those are the ways you decide upon a mate."

He chuckled softly. "I pity McCloud."

Hands on hips, she confronted the broad-shouldered Navajo man. "What's that supposed to mean?"

"The bravest horse is the most difficult to break."

She should have been insulted to the depths of her feminist soul. He was comparing her to an animal—a horse, for goodness' sake! Sandra was well enough acquainted with horses to realize that they aren't the brightest creatures on the earth.

And yet, when she looked into the eyes of this strange man who might have been conjured from the depths of her imagination, who might not even exist at all, she felt somehow blessed. "I'm doing the right thing, aren't I?"

"Yes."

He turned and walked away from her. Only then did she see his pinto pony, untethered and drinking water from the slender creek nearby.

"Martin," she called to him.

He turned slowly. His weathered face held the wisdom of earth.

"Martin, will we find the city?" For an instant, she had a premonition of darkness and danger. "Will we be safe?"

"The legend is in your heart. You must listen to the voices of your spirit." He laughed again. "Promise me, Sandra, that you will name your seventh son after me."

"Seven? My seventh son?"

With the athletic grace of a much younger man, he mounted and rode away.

Chapter Twelve

She didn't tell McCloud about the visit of Martin White Horse—partly because she wasn't sure whether she saw him or imagined him and partly because Martin's message was agonizingly repetitive. Trust. Without trust, they wouldn't find the city, wouldn't have a relationship, wouldn't have anything. But Sandra still wasn't sure that she trusted McCloud.

While they settled down for the night, she brought up the big issue, the biggest bone of her contention, the topic she'd avoided since Letty flew her down here and she made her spectacular helicopter entrance. "I want to talk about the investment, McCloud."

"Fine." He was boiling water on his propane stove for some kind of stew. They'd already eaten all the fresh supplies. "What about the investment?"

"My parents aren't the most practical people on earth. That goes without saying. But they've been lucky enough to survive and even to flourish."

"Do you really think that's luck?"

The realization that had been playing at the edge of her consciousness settled upon her. She'd fought it for years, perhaps for all her life, but now she accepted. "You're right. Maybe it wasn't dumb luck. Though their path was different from mine, it was valid." She sighed. "Even admirable."

"It's good to hear you say that."

She stretched and yawned, noticing that the tension in her shoulders was gone, as if a burden had lifted. "Nevertheless, McCloud, you took advantage of them. You took their life savings. How can I ever trust a man who did that to my family?"

He strode to the place beside a cottonwood where he had stacked their gear and began to paw through it. "By now, I thought I'd proved to you that I didn't steal from them. The money was guaranteed to come back to them. I only wanted the use of it for two years."

"Understood. But they lose all the interest."

"It's a gamble. If I make an archaeological find, they will be well rewarded for the rest of their lives. The city of gold might not be King Tut's tomb, but the value is significant. Collectors pay thousands for pots shards. Do you know the price for actual intact artifacts?"

"Still, you should have talked it over with me. And with my brother and sister."

"Your parents are capable of making their own decisions."

"In most things, yes. But contracts fall into my area of expertise. My parents aren't wealthy investors who can afford to throw away half a million dollars. They're artists. They could return from this Africa trip and regret that their assets are not liquid."

He found what he was looking for in the saddlebag and approached her with it. "Your argument is unnecessary, Sandra."

The paper he dropped in her lap was a single page sheet with a check stapled to the top. The check was in her name and the amount was six hundred thousand dollars. The attached sheet of paper, which was not phrased in legal terms, said that McCloud was turning over the responsibility for the investment made by Emma and Thornton Carberry in their own names and in the names of their children to Sandra Carberry, their attorney. If Sandra signed and deposited the attached check, it signified an end to the agreement, and all previous contracts were null and void.

She blinked up at him. "When did you—"

"After we made love by candlelight. I didn't want this investment standing between us."

She swallowed hard. The enormity of his gesture stunned her. "I don't understand. I thought this money was already spent. On land leases."

"I'm not a millionaire, Sandra, but I do have my own cash reserves."

"Six hundred thousand of cash reserves? By giving me this check, are you straining your own finances?"

"A little," he admitted. "But not painfully."

"If I cash this check, what happens to your quest?"

"After we finish in this area—which I'd already leased with other investments—I'll need to find more capital." He cleared his throat. "Finding more money is my problem. Your problem, Sandra, is that if you cash that check, your parents no longer have a share in El Dorado."

She couldn't take her eyes off the check. All those zeros. It would take her a long time in her career to amass this kind of nest egg. When she looked at this check, she could envision a condo and a sports car and a lifetime membership at the Athletic Club.

And freedom. With this much money at her disposal, Sandra wouldn't have to worry about quitting her partnership. She could afford to be a storefront lawyer, refusing clients she didn't want and taking on all those pro bono cases that didn't pay the rent but gave her the satisfaction of seeing that the right thing had been done. Her share of the investment—one hundred thousand dollars—could buy a lot of leeway. "I could set up my own law practice," she said.

"In Denver?"

"Of course, in Denver. That's my home."

"Why?"

"That's where I have an apartment. And my things." She studied the check again, turned it over in her hands, fondled the serrated edges. "I can't believe you brought this along in the desert. This is no way to do business."

"I'm not a businessman."

"I noticed." She rose to her feet, crossed the few yards that stood between them and gave him a hug. "Thank you, McCloud."

When she tried to move away, he was holding her. She felt the marvelous imprint of his body against hers, listened to his voice rumbling deep in his chest. "Do you know what this means, Sandra?"

"I can buy a condo?"

"It means," he said slowly, "that you have no reason not to trust me."

He was right. Whether real or imagined, her conversation with Martin White Horse convinced her that McCloud had not been a party to Martin's manipulations at the law firm. And McCloud had given her a touching and valid reason for his fifth of May visit. Now this. The check. She had no reason to hold back.

Tilting back her head, she looked up at him. A warmth flowed between them like sweet honey. Her lips parted. Her eyes closed, waiting for his kiss. But he released his embrace and returned to the pot on the propane stove.

Sandra stood apart from him, bereft and baffled. What was wrong now? Surely they had no reason to stay apart. Tonight she would bring him into her tent. Tonight she would experience the wonder of his skillful lovemaking. "Are you angry?"

"No." He turned the spoon over to her. "You cook. I'll tend the horses."

He left her tending their stew and walked away from their camp. He wasn't angry, but he wasn't feeling all that good, either. When McCloud wrote out that check, he had thought that he wanted to appease this woman. But now it didn't feel right.

The problem wasn't the money. It had never been money.

He wanted her to believe in him. There was a perverse corner in his brain that thought she would rip up the check and tell him that she believed in his quest, that she was willing to take the risk. To make the commitment to him. Instead, she wanted to return to Denver and take on a whole different form of law practice. She couldn't wait to leave him, couldn't wait to buy a condo and a car and all the expensive toys that went along with her career.

He stared up at the stars, wishing he could find appeasement in the celestial heavens. She didn't believe in him. The disappointment caused a heavy ache in his chest.

They ate their evening meal in silence.

After they'd cleaned up, she went into her tent and he stretched out on his bedroll on the hard earth. McCloud welcomed the night chill, but it was not cold enough to quench the burning question he felt in his heart. Why didn't she believe him?

Inside her black tent, Sandra tossed and turned, unable to find a restful position on her surprisingly comfy air mattress. The occasional nickering of the horses seemed incredibly loud and disruptive to her rest. And the wind, though she knew it was only a whisper, sounded like a banshee scream.

Her mind should have been completely at ease. After all, she'd won. Her parents' money had been returned in full. And that was what she had been after all the time. Not only that, but Sandra herself would receive a hundred-thousand-dollar windfall, enough to plot out her future in law without considering financial necessity.

Her relationship with McCloud also seemed to be under control. Finally he was treating her with the professional respect that she deserved. But there was something horribly wrong. He was out there, and she was in here. Alone and lonely. Desire shot through her like a command: *Go to him.*

It was only a few paces. If she listened hard, she could hear him breathing. And she desperately wanted to be with him, to feel his arms around her, to taste his mouth, to see that special light in his incredible turquoise eyes.

Why didn't he want her? Why? Finally they'd cleared the hurdle of trusting, and now there was something else, some other obstacle she could only guess at.

This quest, she thought. Sandra mulled the word over in her mind. This search. This journey.

And, in a flash of insight, she knew what was wrong.

Sandra crept through the tent flap. Her eyes were accustomed to the dark, and she spotted McCloud's bedroll just a few yards to the left. He was almost completely hidden by the sleeping bag. Only his thick black hair was showing. She knelt down beside him and gave him a small nudge. "McCloud? Are you awake?"

"Yes." His voice was muffled, but alert.

"Couldn't sleep, could you? Well, I'm not surprised."

"What?"

"I know what you're trying to pull," she said. "And it won't work."

"What the hell are you—"

"I was lying in my tent, thinking, and I've finally got it all figured out."

He rolled to a sitting posture, and the soft folds of the sleeping bag fell to his waist, revealing his naked chest. She longed to touch him, to feel that warm muscular flesh, but Sandra plowed straight ahead.

"You were trying to trick me," she said. "But I'm not going to fall for it."

She stormed back to her tent and found the check and the one-page agreement that he'd given to her. When she returned, McCloud was still sitting up. His gaze rested upon her, glittering with heat. Anger? Or something else? She wished she could test his expression. If she glided her fingers down his shoulders, if she pressed her lips against his mouth, how would he respond? Would he make love to her? She didn't dare think about it.

"I was lying in my tent, McCloud. And I was thinking. You've been on this search for eight years. Is that correct?"

"Don't cross-examine me, Sandra."

"Sorry. It's just a habit." She plunked down beside him, cross-legged on the cold earth. "For some reason, you believe that your quest is nearly at an end. Also, Martin White Horse believes it."

"How do you know what Martin believes?"

"He came here today. At least, I think he came here. I was kind of drowsy, and he just popped up from nowhere. Like a dream, so I'm not sure whether I imagined him or if he was actually here."

"Sandra, what in the hell are you rattling on about?"

"This!" She flapped the paper like a fan. "This agreement! You thought you were pulling a fast one, but it's not going to work." Her logic raced ahead. "We are on the verge of finding the city of gold. It might be tomorrow. Maybe the next day. But it will be found."

"Oh?"

"You believe that, don't you?"

"Hell, yes. But I've believed in this search for a long, long time. I don't get my hopes too high, and I wouldn't advise you to, either."

"What about Martin White Horse? What about the fact that I'm here with you, fulfilling some part of the legend?"

"I suppose you think this is logical."

"Well, of course. With all your experience, you think we're on the verge of finding this place. And

Martin, with his ancient knowledge, he thinks we'll find it." She sat back on her heels. Her voice rang with triumph. "That's why you gave the money back. You want to keep all the gold for yourself."

"Dammit, Sandra."

In the moonlight, she discerned only a glimmer of his full anger, and that glimpse was more intimidating than a full sunlit view. Still, she continued, "Really, McCloud. You didn't return the money just to please me. Nobody—not even you—would make such an extravagant gesture."

She jabbed an accusing finger at his chest. "You're trying to pull a fast one. Well, it's not going to work."

"Do you really believe that? In your heart?"

For a single moment, she still held back, listening to the rapid beating of her own heart and the pressured drawing of breath from her lungs. She wanted to topple into his arms, to trust him implicitly, to believe every golden word he spoke to her. She wanted to follow her instinct rather than rely on facts and logical reasoning. But Sandra had spent her whole life in consideration of rational arguments. She was an attorney, trained to discover answers from fact. She must not listen to her irresponsible heart.

She held the contract and the check before her. "Here's what I think of your gesture, McCloud."

Deliberately, she tore the contract and the check in half. Then in quarters. Then in smaller bits until it was nothing but scraps of paper that would blow on the desert wind to the four corners of the earth.

"There," she shouted. "It's done. And now we find the city of gold."

THE NEXT TWO DAYS of searching passed in a haze. During the day, they rode and walked through canyons and valleys. At night, they avoided physical contact. Sandra slept alone in her tent. McCloud stayed outside, under the stars.

At midmorning of the day they were to start back toward the ranch to replenish their supplies, they had come almost to the end of what appeared to be a box canyon. Sandra and McCloud walked, side by side, with the horses trailing behind them.

Sandra felt terribly low and disappointed. "We could be doing this for the rest of our lives."

"Is that so bad?"

"It's not the land," she tried to explain. "The longer we're out here, the more I enjoy this landscape."

"Not boring?"

"Oh, not at all."

She'd discovered the most precisely refreshing moment of the dawn, when the sun burned away the chill and she could shed her Levi's and wear shorts. And their lunchtime breaks had become a lazy hour when she could lie on a rock like a lizard. Her skin had tanned to a toasty brown. And her body, Sandra knew, had never been more toned. She was flourishing in this high plains desert.

Striding away from him, she went to a small fissure in the rocky face of the canyon wall. There, on a small clump of grass, a small succulent grew. The cactus flower was a deep rich purple. These tiny natural surprises delighted her. In lighter moments, she thought of McCloud and herself as Adam and Eve in the Garden.

"The only thing I really miss about civilization is being unable to take a long hot bath. Or a shower. Oh, a shower would be ecstasy."

"Then what's the problem?"

"It's all this searching. I'm a goal-oriented person, and it drives me crazy to think we might go home empty-handed."

"Thinking about your share of the cash again?"

"Of course. But it's more than that. I like having an ending, a completion. I don't know how you have the patience to search and search and never to find anything."

"The goal, for me, is the search itself. I've enjoyed this. Having you with me has made it different."

Much different, he thought. Though he had not touched her delectable body, her presence pleased him. He looked forward to their quiet moments of talking when her quick mind darted from one topic to another. And she seemed to be growing more beautiful every day. The longer they stayed out here, the more acclimated she became. Her riding skills improved. Her energy increased.

He watched her long firm legs, climbing over rocks. Her sun-browned arms were graceful and sure. And the tawny color of her skin, topped by her thick blond hair, made her just about the finest woman he'd ever seen.

"Being in the desert agrees with you," he said. "You look good, Sandra. Better."

"What does that mean? Before we came out here, I looked bad? Like an ugly pale-faced hag?"

"That was a different kind of pretty. Soft as satin. Delicate." He grinned. "Like the skin on your bottom."

"I have a delicate bottom?"

"A paleface bottom." He caught up with her. "But maybe I ought to take another look, to be sure."

"I'll thank you to keep your paws off my delicate, white buttocks, McCloud."

He paused. "Do you hear that? A kind of rushing sound?"

She listened. Her hopes raised. Maybe they were going to find something after all. Maybe after all this searching, they would locate the city of gold. "I hear it."

There was a break in the canyon wall with sandy-colored rocks piled high on each side. And a stream of water cut a narrow swath in the soil at their feet.

Telling herself not to be too hopeful, Sandra followed him into the irregular jagged cut. The creek widened, rushing across worn surfaces of stone. "Where does this water come from? It can't be run-off from the mountains."

"It's an underwater river. Or a spring. This land is honeycombed with them."

They rounded a tall rock and discovered the source of the water. A natural pool had formed at the edge of the cliff on an overhanging rock. Water slipped over the edge, forming a crystalline waterfall, a curtain of water that was four feet wide.

"Beautiful," she said, covering her disappointment that they hadn't found the source of their quest. Her breast heaved with a sigh, and she accepted the miracle they had found.

"Must be an underground spring."

He climbed up the wall of rocks until he stood level with the pond. It was only about four feet by eight, but it sparkled in the sun like a liquid jewel.

McCloud lifted his arms toward the sun. "Sandra speaks and the land obeys."

"What are you babbling about?"

He held out his hand and pulled her onto the top level. "You said you wanted a bath." He gestured to the pool. "Here it is."

Delighted, she looked down at the water. It was too good to be true. "But this isn't a warm bath."

He scooped his hand in the water and flung the droplets toward her. "Unfortunately, madam, this pond is cold. Heated by the sun before it flows down the creek, but not warm."

"I hate to nitpick a miracle, but it would have been nice to locate a hot spring."

He went to the edge of the cliff. "I'm going to take care of the horses. You stay here and take your bath."

"Really?" Warm or cold, it would be pure luxury to sluice water over her dusty body. "But do we have time?"

"We're not punching a clock."

He eased himself down the hill, leaving her alone at the water's edge. Sandra shucked off her socks and hiking boots. Cautiously, she poked her toe in the water. The temperature wasn't seductively steamy. Nonetheless, she welcomed the chance to clean herself.

She called down to him. "I need a towel and my shampoo."

"Just like a female," he teased. "We locate a pristine artesian spring, and the first thing you do is pollute."

"I will not." Her tone was self-righteous. "All my soaps and lotions are one hundred percent natural. Even the fragrance is a pure essence."

"Terrific. Pretty expensive stuff?"

"Very. And don't you dare give me a hard time about the irony of pure ingredients, easily found in nature, that cost more than chemicals."

"Wouldn't think of it."

He tossed up the towel, a bottle of shampoo and soap.

She stripped. Taking a deep breath, she waded into the pond. In the deepest part, it was only up to mid-thigh and she bobbed under the water. It felt wonderful, only slightly colder than the swimming pool at the Athletic Club. She bobbed again and again, playing, throwing up a fine spray of sparkling diamond droplets.

She lathered her hair and rinsed with the natural rush of water carrying away the suds. This was more clean than she'd felt in days. The cold water tingled on her skin as she ducked under the water again.

When she broke the surface, McCloud was standing there. She noticed that he was carrying his rifle, and a shiver of fear went through her. "What's wrong?"

"Nothing."

He set the rifle down, took off his hat and squatted down beside the pool. His turquoise gaze was hot, and Sandra was terribly aware of her nakedness. Not embarrassed. That would have been foolish because she had made love to this man before. But she was aware of the tautness of her breasts, just below the liquid surface. Her body tingled, and she wished they could make love. Right now. Right here on the sun-warmed rocks.

Did he want the same thing? Is that why he climbed back up here? "McCloud, what do you want?"

"You."

A shiver went through her. Suddenly the pool seemed as warm as a bath.

"But that's not why I came up here," he said. His voice was husky. "I've got to rush you, Sandra. There's a rainstorm gathering in the skies, and I want to be settled down before it hits."

"Can't we stay here?"

"No shelter. Not for us or the horses."

He turned and strode away from her.

With a sigh, she dragged herself back to the reality of their search.

As McCloud had promised, the skies grew more and more overcast. But before the cloudburst hit in late afternoon, they'd made camp.

The roar of thunder rolled across the plains. The dark clouds crackled with lightning. When the first drops began to fall, they crept inside the tent.

"This weather will slow us down," she said.

"Doesn't really matter, so long as we head back to the ranch pretty soon. We're almost out of food."

A sharp pain wrenched her gut. She hadn't thought about the end of the search. "Then I have to go home to Denver."

"We'll make a couple more day trips, but then the quest is over. Your part of it, anyway."

Surprisingly, she didn't want to leave him. She wanted to stay out here forever. Maybe tomorrow they would find something. And, as for tonight... "I can't throw you out in this weather," she said. "If you want to stay here in the tent, it's all right with me."

"Are you asking me to spend the night with you?"

Outside the tent, a thunderclap exploded. "Yes, McCloud. Stay with me tonight."

Chapter Thirteen

Because of the rain, he thought. She invited him into her tent because of the rain. And he could lie on his sleeping bag beside her, watching the rise and fall of her breath. But he wouldn't be allowed to touch. *Not good enough.* The next time they shared sleeping quarters, it would be because she wanted him there, as a man. "I'll step out in a minute," he said, "this is only a spring rain."

"No, McCloud. Spring rain is pitter-patter and splash, splash. This is a typhoon."

"We have the same kind of weather you get in Denver. In the winter there's bitter cold and the occasional blizzard. In springs and summer we have heavy rain, lightning, thunder."

"Tornadoes?"

"Not usually, but don't get me started on this. Weather is important for me, for all ranchers and farmers."

"And searchers," she said. "You have to plan your search time around the weather. Damn, I hate to give up."

"You don't have to, Sandra." His voice was low and gentle, a soothing contrast to the violence of the storm outside. "There's no rule that says you have to leave in two weeks and return to Denver."

"I promised Mr. Jessop—"

"Excuse me if I'm wrong, Sandra, but Jessop is the guy who insisted that you come out here. Whether you wanted to or not. Right or wrong, he said it was a duty of partnership. Do you owe him your loyalty?"

"Of course. He hired me. He promoted me to partner."

"But you earned it."

"Yes, I did. My billable hours are the highest in the firm." She thought of that dignified old attorney, Laurence Jessop, struggling to draw each breath. She didn't want to end up like him—strangled by her own success. "But I can't just quit. What would I do?"

"We need a good attorney down here. You remember Pablo talking about the renegades. Even if the sheriff is capable of rounding up the bad guys, they get off on legal technicalities. The people down here need law and order. They want it. You could have your own practice."

"That would be crazy," she calmly pointed out. "I returned the nest egg to you, broken and scrambled, which means I need to support myself. How could I do that in this area? I'd be giving up thousands and thousands of dollars in income."

"Maybe we'll find the city of gold. We could search every weekend."

He held out his dream to her, and Sandra was tempted to snatch it with both hands. So impractical! Such fantasy!

"You'd like being your own boss," he said. "Taking only the cases you wanted to take. Practicing law by your standards, not to satisfy the client with the most cash."

It sounded wonderful and pure. "I can't believe I'm saying this . . . but I'll think about it."

He took her hand. "I'll be your first client."

"Well, that cinches it," she said sarcastically. "Who needs millionaires and giant corporations when I could have a buffalo rancher as my number-one client?"

"I'm sure Martin White Horse would rather work with a local person than with Jessop, Feldner and White."

"Sweet revenge." She grinned. "I'd love to steal that account from Max the Ax. Of course, I wouldn't do that. It's totally unethical."

"Guess you'll have to settle for me."

"Then I guess we'd better do something to make you a rich man, McCloud. Let's find that city of gold. I have the map right here."

She dug around in a pouch that held her makeup and lotions.

"Not the map," he groaned. "Every night we've studied that map from every direction and every angle, and there's still nothing. No special message."

"I'm sure there's something we're missing."

Spreading it out between them, she poured over the creased sheet of paper that depicted topography. She stabbed with a finger, locating the canyon where they'd found the artesian well. An extremely close scrutiny, using her battery-powered lamp, revealed a tiny shimmer that might have been the pond. She frowned and looked up at him. "I never would have expected to find that pond on this map."

He nodded. "During winter a couple of years back, I used a viewing machine to blow up the photos. It was an improvement. The topography was fairly clear."

"But you found nothing significant."

"Nothing."

She rattled the page. "There's something here. I feel it. Maybe a natural shape."

"Now wouldn't that be handy," he said wryly. "A big arrow in the topography that said 'Search here.'"

"Stranger things have happened. Like those giant petroglyphs in Mexico that can only be seen from the air. Or those circles that are drawn in wheat fields."

"Not the alien spaceships again."

"That's no more farfetched than hitching your wagon to a legend."

"Possibly not. But searching canyons feels more productive than waiting for interplanetary communications."

Dutifully, with black squares, she blanked out the canyons where they had searched. "There's something we're missing. Some clue."

"I've stared at those maps forever, Sandra. And believe me, there's nothing there."

"We need the big pictures," she said. She found the huge representation of the search area. Though the map illustrated an area of several hundred miles, it was smaller than the topographical map. And less detailed. On this fourteen-by-sixteen page, she could see the sweep of highways and the squiggles of creeks. There were indications of small towns, and the cities of Alamosa and Raton looked like giant centers of population. Again, she marked off the area they'd searched. This time, she used a small black marker pen. Her gaze caught on the marked-off areas that had been searched. "You're going from west to east," she said. "Why?"

"The western side seemed more likely as a search area. The legend talks about high walls, and those are found near the mountains."

"So, the farther east you go, the less likely that you'll find anything."

"Not necessarily. Lower elevations have more hospitable weather, which makes them a likely site for a city."

"Show me." She pushed the map toward him. "Show me the route you've been following."

Though the tent was not crowded, he moved close to her. His left arm braced against her shoulders, and Sandra tensed with awareness. Humidity from the rain laced the air with sultriness. She'd done such a good job of suppressing her desires. And yet, when he was near, physical sensation overwhelmed her. Sandra forced herself to concentrate as, with his right hand, he slowly traced his progress. "I started here."

His fingers drew a straight line through the blackened areas on the map. "I went up one side of this valley and down the other. Then I moved to this one."

Up and down. Up and down. When he reached the area they were currently searching, his finger took a different motion. A circle. "On this high plain, I've gone around one side. We're almost here at the northernmost point of the circle, then we'll come around this edge."

Something clicked inside her brain. "Do that again."

He drew a circle. "But that's not really the search pattern, as you know. We're following the main path of a circle, then we radiate out, searching each canyon."

"Like the rays of the sun. A big circle with sawtoothed, jagged rays coming out of it."

"Right."

An insight wavered at the edge of her consciousness, just beyond her comprehension. She turned over the map and pointed to a scribble in the corner. "Like this?"

"Roughly."

"That's odd. I've been making that design for days. Every time I think of the legend, I'm reminded of sun god worship, and I've been doodling a little sun picture. Sometimes I've given it arms and legs. A primitive sketch. Do you think it means anything?"

"It could."

She glanced up at him, and her gaze locked with his. Sandra felt herself sinking, being drawn into his eyes. It took an effort of willpower to look away from him.

Outside the tent, she was aware that the rains had slowed to a light pattering. The night was cool but not cold. A perfect night to spend in his arms.

McCloud cleared his throat. "Go ahead, use your finger and draw your little doodle pattern on the map."

Roughly following the search route he'd taken, she traced the pattern. "But it goes like this. And I always start here. At the top. At the northernmost point."

"That's an area I'd be covering on my next trip out."

"Let's go there tomorrow," she said. "Skip past these other canyons and go to the apex. There's something there."

He could feel it, too. In the taut pull of her shoulders. He could see the possibility in the shimmer of her eyes. And he heard a mystical call in her voice.

"McCloud, it's like I've dreamed this." A shimmering excitement began to build from inside her. She felt strangely detached, separated from the physical desires of her body that urged her toward him. There was another destiny. A golden dream. "I can't remember the dream. But the sensation is there. On the edge of my subconscious memory."

"I believe you," he said. "Tomorrow we go there."

"And tonight..."

He leaned forward and lightly kissed her forehead. "Tonight, we will dream of El Dorado."

He stood, placed his black hat on his head and slipped outside through the tent flap.

She exhaled a breath she hadn't been aware of holding. Her hand, on her breast, felt the fluttering of her heart. If he had wanted to make love on this rainy night, she would have consented gladly. But he had not asked. She'd offered her tent, but he had chosen not to stay with her.

And so, Sandra thought, she would spend the night alone with passion unrequited and dreams unfulfilled.

THE DAWN CAME BRIGHT and clear, but McCloud insisted that there was rain in the air. And Sandra was sensitive enough to the climate that she recognized the drop in temperature. They saddled up their horses, and with an attitude of excitement, they rode past several canyons, circling northward.

At midmorning they reached the area to be searched: a huge canyon with a trickle of a creek sliding down the center. The vegetation, after the rainfall, was lush and green.

Suspense made Sandra giddy as a goose. She hopped down from her horse, Sugar, and pointed triumphantly to a clump of bushes. "Berries. See, there are berries."

McCloud dismounted. "Actually, these are chokecherries."

"They're edible and they look like berries, McCloud. Don't quibble."

"I hope you're right. But this could be a dead end, like all the other dead ends."

"But it won't be."

Her eyes glittered with the most beautiful hope he'd ever seen. In spite of all her denials, this woman was an idealist, a dreamer. She didn't belong in the steel-and-concrete canyons of Denver. She belonged here with him. "Sandra, I—"

"Don't talk. We're going to find it. Today we're going to find the city of gold."

But it wasn't an easy trail. The chokecherry bushes were not only abundant, they were an obstacle. Sandra and McCloud had to pick their way carefully along a narrow, almost-nonexistent path.

Without knowing the source of her knowledge, she said, "The city will be on the west wall so the first rays of sunlight can touch the walls."

"That's very likely. Many Native American abodes are arranged to receive first sun."

"Yes, I must have heard you say that." But she knew that she'd never heard that bit of information before. "Facing the sun. The rising sun."

As they slowly went deeper into the canyon, Sandra stumbled over a ridge in the earth. She knelt down to touch the rugged indentation. "This almost looks like it was carved out."

She touched the side of the ridge, and a shiver went through her. Though the soil had eroded over years and years, she imagined that she could feel the mark of a shovel. She looked up at him. "An irrigation system?"

His hand covered hers, pressing her palm against the sun-warmed earth. "There might have been fields here. Cultivated fields."

"And you couldn't see anything from the aerial photos because of these bushes."

They trailed farther and farther into the wide canyon, not stopping for lunch, not pausing for words. Her gaze scanned near the top of the canyon, following the irregular jutting of rock. Overhead, a hawk swooped and circled. Blue Hawk, she remembered. McCloud's nickname. Sandra concentrated on the graceful flight of the predator bird as it disappeared behind an outcropping of stone.

Leading her horse, she came around the other side.

Her gaze, seeking the flight of the hawk, swept the high walls of the rugged cliffside. And she saw it. The city of El Dorado.

Without speaking, her hand rose toward it. Not pointing, but reaching as if to grasp the legend that had eluded searchers for hundreds of years. El Dorado.

A shout burst from her. "McCloud! It's here!"

The city perched a full thirty feet from the canyon floor in a natural cavern that must have been completely hidden from an aerial view by sheltering rocks that formed a roof. Also, the jutting walls of rock obscured other sighting. From any vantage point other than where she was standing, the city would be invisible.

But it was here. For Sandra to find.

In the sunlight, her vision could discern the outline of two towerlike structures, guarding the entrance to the cavern high above them. Sandra knew this was the place they had been seeking. El Dorado. The legendary city of gold. Her pulse raced with excitement. Yet there was another feeling. From her view, the city seemed dark and foreboding. Not golden.

McCloud stood beside her, and she looked up at him. The expression on his face was beautiful. As she watched, a single tear slipped from his turquoise eye and traced a path down his cheekbone.

"The city of gold," she whispered. "Is it the way you'd thought it would be?"

"It's perfect."

But the distant stone walls looked cold to her, as if the houses were inhabited by ghosts and dark forces. There was danger at the brink of this discovery. She sensed the presence of something fearful. "A curse. McCloud, have you ever heard of a curse on this place?"

"Only that it's never been found."

"Maybe we should come back later." That sounded right to her. "Come back later with Martin White Horse and some other people, archaeologists."

"And leave here?" He was shocked at the idea. "Without going up there and looking around?"

"It doesn't seem safe."

Though there wasn't a cloud in the sky, a dark shadow passed across her consciousness. Once she took this step there would be no chance for turning back.

"The cellular phone," she said. "We can make camp here, and I'll telephone Martin and tell him where we are, and he can bring the proper climbing gear."

His refusal was adamant. "I've spent eight years searching for this city, and I'll be damned if I'm not the first person who sets foot on that land."

Sandra held back her objections. Her nervousness paled in comparison to his muscular determination. Her will was not strong enough to stand against his after years of searching.

Softly he said, "I'd like you to come with me. To experience the city for the first time."

She hesitated. Every sensible urge in her body warned against going up into that city. It was dangerous. The stones were likely to crumble. She could be trapped there. But when he took her hands and lightly kissed her forehead, her premonitions faded. "Please, Sandra. I won't let anything happen to you."

He was asking her to trust him. Perhaps, she thought, to trust him with her life. And she had to agree. For this was the course her life would follow, trusting and believing in McCloud.

She set her jaw firmly. "How do we get up there?"

"Climb." The cliff was not sheer, and several handholds were easily visible. The city itself was only thirty feet above the canyon floor. But there was a thrusting lip that would be difficult to negotiate.

Gritting her teeth to keep from nagging, Sandra asked, "Have you done this before? I'm really not giving you a hard time, McCloud, but are you a good enough climber to handle this?"

"I'm not bad." He rigged a climbing harness with an array of nylon ropes, chocks and nuts to wedge into fissures in the rocks.

"What about pitons?" she asked. "Don't you need pitons and belaying ropes?"

"This isn't the Alps, Sandra. Just a little cliff, an easy ascent. I'll get up there, secure a rope and then I'll come down to help you."

"I won't need help, thank you. I can climb a rope," she said. "If it's such an easy ascent and all."

"Good. Take care of the horses while I climb."

She watched him vault up the first fifteen feet with ease. Then he slowed. The next five feet took ten minutes to climb, as he placed chocks to give himself something to cling to.

Sandra was unable to stand helplessly and watch while he climbed. Busily, she tended the horses, pulling off saddles and packs. She allowed them to browse free in the thick grasses of the canyon.

Peeking back at the cliff, she saw McCloud, dangling from a tiny, precarious handhold. She covered her mouth to contain a cry of fear. Overreacting, Sandra told herself. McCloud seemed to know what he was doing. At least, he hadn't fallen.

From where she stood at the base of the cliff, the city was barely visible within its cavern. What had it been like when people lived there? Did they climb up and down ladders to reach their homes? The placement of the structure made it virtually impregnable, she thought. A perfect hiding place for a peaceable tribe of mainly women and children.

If this was the golden city of legend, it had been a haven with plentiful growth in this lush canyon. A safe place for the children, a nurturing place. Yet Sandra's apprehensions grew stronger as McCloud neared the overhanging ledge just below the city's cavern. Keeping an eye on him, Sandra dug through her packs. She found her cellular phone, and she fastened it on the belt she'd bought in Santa Fe. From the hooks, she fastened a flashlight, the flare gun, her Swiss army knife, her hunting knife and a canteen, as well as other items.

McCloud slipped over the ledge to safety, and relief swept through her. He was safe.

He reappeared, both arms raised over his head in a victory salute. This, she thought, was how she would always remember him. Brave and strong, claiming his dream. To dream was good, but to achieve... That, Sandra thought, was better by far.

He tossed down a rope and descended quickly rappelling down the cliff face, using a climbing harness. She was standing, waiting for him, shivering with an unexplainable fear. With a loud whoop of excitement, he grabbed her in his arms and swung her off her feet in a high circle.

"You're magical, Sandra. You said it would be here, and it was! The city. It exists!"

In spite of her fears, she was chuckling. "Of course it exists. You never thought otherwise, did you?"

"Hell, yes."

"McCloud, put me down."

He released her and proceeded to enact a victory dance, leaping and shouting. With both her feet planted on the earth, she frowned in the face of his wild excitement. "Are you sure we should be mucking around on this site? Is it safe?"

"I won't put you in danger, Sandra."

"Is that something you can judge?" Her foot tapped nervously on the ground. She squinted at him. "You don't look particularly rational."

"What about you? You're the one who found this place. You're the one who had the mysterious instinct. You led me here, Sandra."

And she wasn't altogether delighted about that. She just couldn't shake this sense of impending disaster, the dark clouds that had gathered in the back of her mind. "Okay, McCloud, I'll trust you to watch out for my safety. But, just in case, I am taking my cellular phone."

"By all means," he said seriously.

He hitched her into a climbing harness and showed her how to feed the ropes through. "This would be easier," he said, "if you'd take some of that gear off your belt."

"Not a chance."

"Do you really need all that stuff? We're only going to be up here for a little while, just a brief look-see."

"I'm taking every piece of equipment I can get my hands on," she said obstinately. "And if I had more, I'd take that, too. I want to be prepared."

"Fine." He backed up a pace. "There are little chock blocks to brace your feet against. But they won't be much good up on top. I'll give you a hand up on the last ledge."

Thus saying, he ascended ahead of her. "Watch where I'm stepping," he instructed. "This really won't be hard."

And it wasn't. She braced the rope behind her and climbed, catching slowly and carefully, stepping from one chock to another. As he had promised the ascent was simple until she reached the last little bit before the top. Using the rope, she braced her feet and climbed around it while he pulled her into his arms.

"We're here, Sandra. Let's go."

"Wait." Before taking a step toward the stone structures, she pulled the rope up behind her, stopping only when it lay coiled at her feet.

McCloud watched her with interest. "Why did you do that?"

"I have no idea." She shrugged. "It just seemed like the right thing to do."

"Definitely the right thing," he murmured, "if you happen to be a cliff dweller from five or six hundred years ago."

"That's how old this is. Amazing." Sandra had already begun to walk toward the two- and three-storey stone buildings. Their walls seemed patchworked together with a thick plaster.

"Sandra, you brought the rifle."

"And shells, too."

"Why? This place has been relatively undisturbed for centuries. What do you expect to find here?"

She wasn't sure, but the tension had not left her, and Sandra did not want to be caught unawares. She sauntered toward the city. "Remarkable that it's still standing."

"It's sheltered here," he pointed out. "Even more than the other cliff dwellings that have been found."

And there were other differences. This city was built more deeply into the cavern. Only two buildings stood at the front entry. Both were three stories tall, and they gave the appearance of sentry towers. The doors on each had rotted open.

As Sandra paused at the entrance, McCloud was struck with a memory that wasn't a memory. He imagined her, Sandra, dressed in white, almost a togastyle garment, but he realized that it was white leather, bleached to purity by the sun. Her hair was blond, sparkling with a light of its own, with the pure fire of the dawn.

"Is it safe to go inside?" she asked.

He blinked. She was Sandra again,. Was it safe? The mood of this place was affecting him. The lure of ancient dust swirled in the air, bringing visions of another time. And the whistle of arid breezes sounded like a siren's cry.

"I don't know, McCloud. Some of these walls look like they're crumbling." She reached toward the wall, then drew her hand back suddenly, as if she'd been burned. Her eyes were wide as she faced him. "I'm sorry. I shouldn't touch anything, right? I might mess up some kind of archaeological find."

He stepped up beside her, half expecting her to disappear. If she were part of the dream, part of the dreaming, she would vanish. But that was crazy. He'd known her body. Not even a dream could duplicate the intimacy they had shared. When he felt her warmth against him, McCloud squeezed her tightly against his chest. She was as real as he was. Not a dream. Not a mystic legend.

She clung to him, but all the ridiculous implements on her belt made their embrace clumsy. And he laughed. Nothing with this woman would be simple, but everything would be exciting.

"We'll explore carefully, Sandra. And you're right not to touch anything. I don't think we'll mess up an archaeological find, but we might dislodge the brick that's holding this place together."

He stepped cautiously into the sentry tower and she followed.

"Sandra, look!" He picked up a circular object, about the size of a dinner plate, from the floor. It was coated with hundreds of years of dust, but the shape was unmistakable. A round sun-shaped face with sharp points radiating out from it. McCloud traced his finger across the surface, revealing a face. Eyes and tongue and lips. It was a mask, and it was made from pure soft gold.

She dropped to her knees beside him. "It really is a golden city."

"This is unbelievable. We must be the first people to have found this city. The first ones. Otherwise this mask would be gone."

"Do you think there are other artifacts?"

"I can't wait to look. Sandra, this really is a dream come true. It's like Carter discovering King Tut's tomb."

"Should we go any deeper? Maybe we need to notify somebody."

"This is my dream. And yours. We'll explore at our leisure before we call in the Navajo and the Ute tribes. And the U.S. government and the Colorado State Historical Society people."

She frowned. "Are you expecting problems?"

"Let me put it this way. Nobody much cared if I searched until I had a gray beard down to my knees. But finding the city of gold puts a whole new light on things. The Native Americans have a claim to this area as a sacred site, and the state government could designate it a park." He took her hand and laced his fingers with hers. "I could use a good lawyer."

She beamed. "You've got one, baby."

"And what do you advise?"

"Let's take a look around. Carefully, though. This city still makes me feel creepy."

Beyond the twin sentry towers, the houses were all one and two stories with low ceilings and doorways that McCloud had to duck into. Though many of the household goods had been left behind, they found no more golden objects.

At the deepest part of the cavern was a sprawling one-story house with several rooms attached one to another. McCloud counted. "Seven. There are seven rooms in a row."

"I don't suppose Snow White ever visited."

"Not a deeply archaeological attitude, Sandra."

"Well, I'm not a deep archaeologist."

They paused outside what appeared to be the main entry to the largest room. Unlike most of the houses where the wooden doors had deteriorated to crumbling planks, this doorway still hung on its hinges. But it stood slightly ajar, inviting them to enter. Though it should have been dark at this depth in the cavern, this house had been situated in such a way that the sunlight reached the face of the main wall, and the stones seemed to glitter as if they were sprinkled with gold dust.

McCloud opened the door and the sunlight shone inside in a long rectangle. The air was still. Utter silence greeted them. There was a sense of something momentous about to happen.

"Sandra, do you have a flashlight?"

She unhooked the light from her belt and handed it to McCloud. "It's your dream. Give it light."

He shone the beam into the room. The light reflected and glimmered. Gold.

Chapter Fourteen

Sandra peeked around his shoulder. There were plates stacked in the center of a wooden table. Though the dust lay heavily upon them, the edges shone of gold. Another sun mask hung on a wall opposite the door. On a shelf were a row of statues, similar to the Hopi kachina dolls. Through the heavy coat of grime, bits of gold shimmered.

McCloud's voice was reverent. "You're right, Sandra. We better notify somebody. As an archaeologist, I'm in way over my head."

"This is amazing," she said. "Why didn't they take this stuff with them? And why is it all here in this room?"

"Could be a burial ritual," he said. "When the leader of this city died, he—or she—might have been sealed in this house with all his or her possessions. Like the Pharaohs in Egypt."

"Which would mean that we're standing in a tomb." His guess felt right to her. A tomb. That would account for her feeling of dread. They were trespassing on ancient and sacred ground.

"Or this longhouse might have been a place of worship and all the gold was kept here." He picked one of the statuettes off the shelf and weighed it in his hand before brushing the dirt away. "The craftsmanship is fairly primitive, but the damn thing feels like solid gold. There must have been a mine in this vicinity."

"We should leave, McCloud."

"Right." But he stood at the arched door leading to the next room, shining her flashlight on the walls. "There's more stuff in here. A bed. A little gold pot and a dish."

"I'm going, McCloud. Right now."

He turned to her, cocked his head to one side. "This place spooks you, doesn't it?"

"I don't know if it's the place." She felt like running, fleeing from an unnamed terror. "But there's danger. Something is going to happen, something bad."

"You trusted me," he said. "Now I'll trust you. Let's get out of here."

They stepped out of the longhouse into the light and walked along the path that led directly to the entrance between the sentry towers. When the fresh light of day struck Sandra's face, she breathed more easily. Near the edge of the cliff where she'd neatly piled the rope, she sat.

McCloud held out his hand. "Give me the cellular phone. Hopefully, I can make a few connections and we'll stay right here until they arrive."

"Stay here?" Suppressed panic made her voice shrill. "Not here, please. I can't spend the night here. I'll be awake the whole time, waiting for the ghostly hand of Dawn Fire to rest on my shoulder."

"Okay, we'll go to the valley. Now give me the phone."

She detached the phone from her belt and passed it to him. "There. Aren't you glad that I brought all this junk?"

"You were brilliant." He turned on the phone. "But this thing is full of static. Does it work?"

"I kind of banged it on my way up here."

He punched out a number on the phone. Barely able to hear the voice on the other end, McCloud left a detailed message on Martin White Horse's answering machine. Then he held the phone, considering who should be his next contact. Considering all the years he'd been searching, it seemed odd that he hadn't decided on a direct course of action once the city was found. Since he'd never planned to carry the spoils away with him, he hadn't brought any means of conveying these treasures. Now that he'd seen them, it was inconceivable to leave them here.

Below them, his horses whinnied and shied. McCloud's gaze scanned the canyon valley. He saw a flash, a metallic shimmer. In reflex, he dropped to a squatting position.

"What is it?" she asked.

He gestured for her to move back into shelter, but Sandra was right beside him. "I thought I saw something."

"Try these." In her hand was a collapsible set of binoculars. McCloud held the lenses to his eyes and searched the thick bushes.

He saw the horses first—sleek animals, saddled up and ready to ride. Four of them. Then he spied the men. They stood in a cluster, staring up at the city. Their handguns were drawn.

"Give me the rifle, Sandra. And get out of the way."

"Use the phone, McCloud. Call Pablo. Call the sheriff."

He picked it up. There was no tone. He shook the instrument hard. "It's not working."

"Sure it is." She took it from him, punched the buttons, flicked the switches. Nothing. The mobile phone was useless as a tin can with a string attached. "I hate this. These things never work when you need them. The only time my car phone went out was when I had a flat tire. I had to fix the tire myself."

This time, McCloud thought, the solution might not be so simple. He lay flat on his belly, peering through the glasses. There were four men, and they weren't bothering to be subtle. One of them had discovered the pile Sandra had made of their supplies.

Sandra stretched out beside him. "What do you see? Who is it?"

"I don't know. Probably the same guys who shot at Letty's helicopter."

There were shouts and laughter below as the renegades opened the saddlebags. It was only a matter of time before these men decided to ascend the cliff and invade the city of gold. McCloud's search had been for nothing. All he had accomplished was to lead thieves to the city. "Damn! Maybe there is a curse."

She managed to raise a static signal on the telephone and punched out the phone number for the ranch. Through the thick fuzzy noise, she heard Pablo's voice. Then the static level overcame human sound. Sandra passed the phone to McCloud.

He held it to his ear, then pulled it away. "I can't hear a damn thing."

"Go ahead and talk. Maybe your voice is getting through."

McCloud gave directions. Quick references on the map that was in his office. The phone sounded like buzzing hornets. He had very little hope that Pablo had heard anything.

He turned it off. "Okay, Sandra. I need to know exactly what you've packed on that miracle belt of yours."

"First-aid kit. Flashlight. A camera. A canteen. Hunting knife and Swiss army knife. A flare gun—"

"Great! How many flares?"

She checked the package that had come with the gun. "Three. And I brought a box of shells for the rifle."

"You're brilliant, Sandra. We can hold these guys off. At least for a little while."

He checked the rifle and cocked it, then lay flat and took aim. Their supplies were piled about twenty-five yards from the foot of the cliff near a grouping of rocks, but McCloud had a clean shot. He could pick off one, maybe two.

As she watched him, her head began to throb. The blood pounded in her temples. "You're not going to shoot them."

"You bet I am." His turquoise eyes were cold and calculating. "I'm not sure if I can hit all of them. But I can get one or two, improve our odds."

"But you can't! That's murder! Killing in cold blood."

"It's them or us, Sandra."

She stretched out on her belly beside McCloud. This couldn't be happening. The fears she had felt since they came to this place were justified. The danger, she realized, was not in haunted stones from an ancient civilization. But here. A present-day threat.

Her jaw clenched. They'd come all this way for nothing. And what about the legend? Dawn Fire and her warrior found safety and succor. They had raised seven sons, had lived happily ever after.

But that was a fairy tale. And McCloud was taking aim.

"Violence," she said, "is never the answer."

His trigger finger relaxed. He turned to her. The hardness in his eyes, a predator's eyes, gentled. "And now the legend is complete. You've warned me—just as Dawn Fire warned the braves around the camp-fire."

As soon as he spoke, the confusion within her stilled. Whether it was coincidence or magic, they had played out almost every turn in the legend. Except for the final commitment.

"McCloud," she whispered. "I love you."

"I love you, too. With all my heart."

The voices below them came closer.

McCloud kissed her with a fierce passion. And then he released her. He rolled to his belly, inched to the rim of the ledge and fired a warning shot.

Sandra stifled a gasp of surprise. The earth beneath her seemed to tremble.

McCloud shouted down to the men. "You got what you want. Now get the hell out of here."

His vantage point was excellent. Even if they spread out to scale the cliff, he would see their approach. But that meant they could also see him. They could settle in and outwait him. In addition to their own guns, they had his other rifle and several more rounds of shells.

As far as McCloud could figure, the only way he and Sandra could escape this city and get away from here alive was to use the same route they'd used to get here, climbing down the wall. They'd be a hell of an easy target.

A shout came from below them. "Climb down. We ain't going to hurt you. We going to help you."

McCloud muttered. "Help us straight to heaven."

He peeked over the edge again. One of the men was lifting his bag full of cooking equipment. McCloud took aim and fired into the canvas satchel.

The man dropped it. He whirled, drew his pistol and fired several times toward the edge of the cliff.

McCloud ducked down.

"I know who you are," the man shouted. "You're that crazy man. McCloud. The guy who's looking for a city of gold."

"Gold?" another questioned. "You think he's got gold up there?"

The sharp report of a pistol sounded. Then another gunshot and another. About a foot from McCloud, a fine spray of gravel kicked up. Sandra screamed.

He turned to her. "Are you all right?"

She nodded.

"Sandra, go back to the city. Go inside one of the houses."

"No." Her eyes were wide. "Can't you feel it?"

The ground beneath them was shuddering. Though the sentry towers behind them stood firm, the stone and ancient mortar might collapse at any moment, shaken by the echo of gunfire.

"McCloud!" came a shout. "You got a woman with you. Let her go. We won't hurt her."

Sandra's breath caught in a gasp. "Oh, God, what are we going to do? We're trapped here."

"We're going to wait." He looked to the skies where dark clouds had begun to gather. "If we have another storm, like the one last night, we might be able to get out of here."

"How?"

"We'll climb down at night. In the dark. They'll be less likely to set a guard in a heavy rainfall. We can make it."

She wasn't so sure. Climbing up a thirty-foot cliff with a safety harness during the daylight was a lot different than sliding down a rope in the dark. On a rainy dark night.

"Maybe we could negotiate with them," she suggested.

"Not a chance." His fist clenched. The muscles in his jaw tightened. "Eight years, Sandra. I've been looking for this place for eight long years. I won't leave it to these jackals."

"What choice do we have? Our only water is what's in the canteen. We won't last two days."

"There might be another way," he said. "A lot of these cliff dwellings have escape exits. If we explore, we might find another way down."

"Okay." That made sense to her. Sandra swallowed her fears. "I'm going to look."

She inched away from the ledge, keeping her head down until she'd reached the walls of the sentry towers. The winds had picked up, weaving through the walls of the city with an eerie moaning, like the voices of those who were long dead. Ghostly voices? A few weeks ago, Sandra would have sneered at the very concept. But that was before she'd spent time in the plains, searching; that was before she accepted the many forces of nature that were beyond her comprehension. There were mysteries in the shifting winds and the rising moon. There were secrets to be revealed, if only she could listen.

Sandra went to the longhouse where they had discovered golden plates and statuettes. Using her flashlight, she went through the first room into the second. There was a bed and a golden vase. Through the third archway, she found a similar chamber, a simple room, like a monk's cell.

On the opposite side, she went all the way to the opposite end, finding nothing. Then she paused, standing very still.

There was the echo of more gunfire. A fine silt drifted down from the ceiling of the ancient dwelling. Then she heard another noise—the unmistakable trickling of water.

Behind this house? She returned to the front and paused at the doorway. The wooden door balanced on its hinges, but she was aware of how fragile these structures were. The stones fitted delicately, one upon the other. In places, the mortar had disintegrated completely. It seemed as if the whole house could collapse with one hard shove.

Cautiously, she circled the longhouse, searching for the source of the trickling noise. If there was a spring, there might be a fissure in the wall, an escape route.

At the farthest corner of the cavern, her flashlight shone on an auric pattern, pressed into the rocks in a frieze. Faces of the sun. Her light flashed to the wall opposite. Faces of the moon. In the center, water oozed between from the rocks and trickled into a stone well. It was filled, nearly to overflowing. Yet the water level did not change.

An artesian well, she thought. But why didn't the water level in the well change? Why didn't it spill over the edges and flood the city?

McCloud would know. She crept back to the ledge where he lay flat, rifle by his side.

As soon as she took a position beside him, he said, "They've taken the horse and all our gear. It looks like they're leaving."

"That's good."

"But unbelievable. If they think there's anything of value here, they'll stick around and wait for us to climb down." He rolled onto his back and looked up at her. "They might even let us get away, Sandra. But they'll rob this place. And I won't be here to stop them."

"It's better than being dead, McCloud."

"If you weren't with me..." He stroked the dust from her cheek. "If I were alone, I'd be tempted to make a stand against them."

"Then I'm glad I'm here. This place. This city of gold is your dream. But no dream is worth dying for."

She told him about the well. Fascinated, he left his sentry post and went with her to see it for himself.

In the dark grotto at the back of the cavern, it seemed that they had entered the most intimate portion of the city.

"The heart," McCloud said. For a moment, he was so intrigued with the mysteries of this civilization that he forgot about the very present danger. "Amazing. This is a very advanced arrangement. What we have here is plumbing."

"Why doesn't the well overflow?"

"The water has to be redirected." Using her flashlight, he searched the edge of the well until he found an earthenware conduit that led to another conduit running along the wall of the cavern. "The overflow feeds into here. Then it travels, probably to another well, and out."

"And this is unusual?"

"Very." He glanced up at the cavern walls. "This water table is high. Sandra, this wall, this whole cliff, has got to be tremendously unstable."

"What does that mean? Earthquakes?"

"Probably. Did you feel tremors?"

She nodded. He could see a reflection of this new fear in her dark eyes, and McCloud wanted more than anything to protect her, to shield her from all the potential disasters that had arisen to mock his triumph in finding the city. He almost would have given away this discovery to reassure her. Almost.

"Is there a danger of an earthquake right now?" she asked.

"I don't know. But these buildings have remained standing for hundreds of years. It seems unlikely that right now at this moment, the earth would—"

"It's not unlikely at all," she said. "From the moment I saw this place, I knew there was danger for us. It was almost like somebody was warning me, and I should have followed that instinct. This city was never meant to be found."

"You can't mean that, Sandra."

"But I do." Her voice rose to a high nervous pitch. When he reached for her, she recoiled from his touch. "Don't pat me on the head and tell me everything will be fine."

"Wouldn't dream of that." His sarcasm was wasted. She was too high-strung, too tense.

He followed her back to the front of the cavern. At the sentry tower, she confronted him. "Even if those men are gone, how will we get back to the ranch without food or horses?"

"We'll walk. It'll take a couple of days, but there's plenty of water out here."

Her fingers clenched into fists and she held them to her forehead. "I hate this. I'm sorry I can't be stronger. But I'm scared. And I'm hungry."

This time, when he pulled her close, she fell against him. As he held her, stroking her back and shoulders, her tension eased. "It's okay, Sandra. We'll make it through this. You and me."

Her body heaved as she fought tears. She refused to start crying like a baby. Not now! "I wish I could be brave."

"You are brave. Don't ever believe that you're not."

"How can you say that?"

"You're making your way in the world. Every day. On your own terms. You were courageous enough to come here, to search. You're not lacking bravery, Sandra."

He kissed her forehead and held her close. The mouth of the cavern showed an angry sky, full of the dark portent of rain. His dream had become a nightmare for her, but McCloud knew they could make it.

The die had been cast, their destiny determined. If he had to choose between protecting the city and protecting Sandra, he would abandon the gold, the artifacts and the fascinating evidence of a culture that was unlike any other in this area. His treasure, he knew, was the life he might share with this woman.

She pulled away from him. When she looked up at him, her determination was clear. "What should we do?"

"Right now, we'll wait. Those renegade bastards haven't left the area. They're waiting for us to climb down. And I want the cover of darkness."

"Until then?"

"We wait."

He left her and crawled on his belly to the overhanging ledge. Focusing the binoculars, he searched every bush, every rock, every tree that could be seen on the canyon floor. There was no sign of anyone else, but McCloud didn't believe it. They were still there.

She crept up beside him. "Do you see them?"

"No."

"Maybe they gave up," she said hopefully. "They might have decided there was nothing up here worth stealing."

As if to refute her, an ominous roar of thunder echoed in the canyon. The danger was not gone.

"Maybe they've left," McCloud said. "But I don't want to be the one dangling from the end of a rope, climbing down this cliff, if you're wrong."

"Good point." She stretched out on her belly beside him. "I'll stay here and keep watch, McCloud. You go ahead and explore the city."

He brightened. "Are you sure you don't want to come with me?"

"Absolutely. I don't want to be near those buildings again."

He didn't need to be asked twice. McCloud reminded her not to stay in one place on the lip of the cliff, making herself a target. She should scan the area, trying to locate the position, if any, that the men had taken. "But don't worry," he said. "I doubt they'll make a charge at the cliff and start climbing, and if they do, you'll hear them."

He dashed off to experience the city he'd dreamt of for so many years. And she settled down to watch the bushes and the trees. Occasionally, she toyed with the cellular telephone, but there was nothing but static on the instrument. All of her careful, high-tech preparations had been for nothing. They were trapped in a situation out of the Old West. And all she could do was lie here and hope the cavalry would suddenly ride over the hill and rescue them. More likely, the Indians, she thought. Martin White Horse had taken such an interest in McCloud's quest, surely, if he received McCloud's telephone message, he would come.

The incongruity of Martin White Horse having an answering machine made her smile, and Sandra took that as a good sign. Her sense of humor was returning. The fearful grasp that had held her since they entered the city seemed to be loosening.

The sunset, this evening, was dismal and dark. And yet, when McCloud finally returned to her side, Sandra caught a glimpse of gold, shooting beneath the underbellies of the clouds. He lay beside her, a contented smile on his face.

"I thought of taking the mask," he said. "I thought I might save that piece. But premonition stopped me."

"Premonition?"

"This city has stood for hundreds of years, untouched. Amazingly, no one has robbed these buildings. It seemed disrespectful to be the first robber."

"But if we get out of here, you plan to open the city to archaeological study, don't you?"

"That's different. If it's time for the city to be discovered, all of these statues and plates need to be here, as they were. Intact." His gaze drifted into the valley. "Any sign?"

"I haven't seen anything," she said, looking out.

"But they're there." He pointed. "Just beyond that ridge. Don't you see the smoke of their campfire?"

She concentrated hard, finally noticing a thin ribbon of smoke that trailed up into the dark skies.

"Didn't you smell it?" he asked.

"I'm a city girl. My nostrils are plugged with smog."

He lay on his side and took both her hands in his. "You've got your attitude back. That's good."

"My attitude?"

"That little chip on your shoulder. It looks good on you."

They stayed at the edge of the cliff, watching and waiting until the starless night surrounded them. The clouds burst, and the rain fell in torrents.

He held her close and whispered. "Are you ready?"

"This is like the first time I came out here. I'm wet and miserable." She brightened a tiny bit. "But so are you."

"Kind of sweet, huh?"

"Right. The couple who gets wet together, stays together."

"And we will stay together, Sandra. When this is over, you're coming to the ranch to live with me."

Before she could protest, he tossed the nylon rope over the edge of the cliff. Their retreat was underway.

"I'll go first," he said. "Cover me."

"Did you just ask me to—"

"The rope is going to be slick," he advised. "When you make your descent, use the climbing harness."

McCloud kissed her, then disappeared over the edge.

Though she could see almost nothing through the pouring rain, she knew he'd run into trouble. There was a shout. The voice was not McCloud's.

"Don't move," the voice shouted again.

"Okay, don't shoot." That was McCloud. Frantically, Sandra tried to see the men. But it was too dark. In this dim light, she couldn't know if she was shooting McCloud or the other man.

"About time," the man said. "There had better be gold up there."

"There's nothing."

"Yeah, sure." His voice lifted. "Hey, lady, you come down now. I got your boyfriend."

"Don't do it, Sandra."

"You shut the hell up."

There was the sound of a scuffle. The rain had begun to thin, and she could see McCloud's tall form struggling with a man who was much smaller.

Sandra made her decision quickly. *Climb down.* The fear she associated with the city had begun to creep into her heart, and she'd rather face a whole horde of bandits than to be trapped in this ancient city.

First she stood on the very edge of the cliff. The man who McCloud was fighting yelled for help. There was no more need to be secretive. Sandra raised the flare gun into the air. She fired into the dark, rainy night. In the momentary illumination, she tried to take aim. But it was still impossible to see what was going on below her. She reloaded the flare, then she heard McCloud, "Hurry, Sandra. Now!"

Bracing herself with the nylon rope, she made it past the lip of the cliff, then quickly descended, half climbing and half falling.

Strong hands grasped her waist and she let out a cry that quickly became relief. "McCloud."

"Nice job of covering me, Sandra. Let's get out of here."

"What happened to—"

"Unconscious."

They cut across the canyon floor, ducking behind bushes. Though the rain had slowed to a gloomy mist, it was still too dark to see anything clearly. They heard the sound of horses as the other renegades entered the canyon. Their leader gave quick commands to find the man who had been watching, to spread out, to locate McCloud and the woman. "Don't forget. They got a gun."

Dodging behind rock and the thick cover of choke-cherry bushes, McCloud and Sandra made their way almost to the mouth of the canyon.

"There's almost no cover out here," he said.

"But we can't stay in the canyon. They'll find us there."

Apparently, the renegades had counted on the terrain to flush out their prey because they had scattered near the canyon's mouth.

McCloud hunkered down behind a rock. He pushed Sandra behind him and raised his rifle, taking aim.

"No," she said. "You can't shoot them."

"How else are we going to get out of here?"

"It's murder."

"Self-defense, Sandra. This is goddamned self-defense."

"McCloud, please don't. We can find another way."

The click of a rifle being cocked behind them ended the argument. They turned and saw the man, looking down the barrel of his rifle. His lips curled in an evil manner. His dark eyes were cold. "Listen to the lady," he said. "You don't want to shoot nobody, man."

McCloud had no choice but to give up his rifle. When he placed it on the ground, the renegade leader stayed a safe distance away from them. There was nothing McCloud could do. To attack this armed man would be suicidal.

"Move," he ordered them.

And Sandra noticed that his attention focused solely on McCloud. He barely glanced in her direction. Could she run? Could she find shelter and...and then what?

The utter hopelessness of their situation wrenched through her like a sob. But she didn't cry.

"I said, 'Move.'" He nudged them forward into the open space at the edge of the canyon. And he called out to his companions. "They're here. I got them. We're over here."

Seeking comfort, she reached for McCloud's hand. But he pulled away from her. His gaze fastened at her belt, and Sandra became aware of all the weapons still at her disposal. On her belt, she wore the hunting knife and the flare gun. But a knife was useless against men with guns. And she couldn't shoot them with a flare.

But she had to try, had to do something. As the other men moved through the shadows of night to surround them, she pulled the flare.

"Hey! What are you doing?"

She held the gun directly over her head and fired off her last flare signal.

The flash of light revealed that they were not alone with the renegades. Not twenty feet away came a row of dark sleek horses, probably ten or twelve. And the men who rode these horses were warriors, each aiming a rifle. They were led by Martin White Horse.

Sandra hadn't heard them coming, hadn't known they were there. It was as if they had materialized from the mysterious night as guardians of the ancient city, coming home to claim their sacred heritage.

Martin White Horse gave a command in Navajo, then repeated it in English. "Throw down your guns, and we will allow you to live."

The young renegades braced themselves angrily, prepared for a battle. But they were ill matched against these warriors on horseback with rifles already aimed. Their leader flung his rifle to the ground with a curse. "Do what he says," he advised the others. "I know this guy and he don't mess around."

While the Navajo men collected the guns and tied the wrists of the renegades, Martin White Horse came to stand beside Sandra and McCloud. He offered her a blanket against the chill, and Sandra gratefully accepted it.

McCloud nodded to him. "It's here, Martin. The city is here."

The old Navajo, tall and proud, looked from McCloud to Sandra. "I knew it would be."

At that moment, as if by magic, the rains stilled. The clouds parted and moonlight bathed the plains in a surreal light that was somehow appropriate to the legend of Dawn Fire.

Martin recounted, "It was a woman who led the people here. She advised against war."

When McCloud looked down at Sandra, his turquoise eyes shone with fond comprehension. "That was why you wouldn't let me fire at these guys."

She shook her head. "No. I've never tried to follow the legend. I've never tried to be Dawn Fire."

And yet the coincidences had mounted to such an extent that she couldn't deny them. When first she rode into the desert, she found McCloud against all odds to the contrary. On the first night, she had interrupted the men, including Martin White Horse and Hank Broken Wing, as they sat around the campfire. The legend of Dawn Fire called upon her to do the same. Also, on that night, Sandra had made love with McCloud, an act that went completely against her better judgment and was so uncharacteristic that she could hardly believe it had happened.

Just as Dawn Fire had left her brave, Sandra had left McCloud.

She looked up at him. "But you never searched for me. The brave who made love with Dawn Fire searched for her."

"The quest," said Martin White Horse, "was within your hearts."

Sandra wrapped her blanket more tightly around her shoulders. "You know, Martin, the legends don't say anything about that sun-ray sketch that I kept playing with and that gave us the last clue to finding the city."

"Very true," McCloud added with a grin. "It occurs to me that there wasn't a word in those legends about cellular phones or answering machines, either." He looked toward Martin. "And that's how you found us. Right?"

He nodded. The moonlight shimmered on his long white hair that contrasted with the strong lines of his face. Though he appeared to be the embodiment of an ancient civilization, his words were relevant to the most modern times. "I have found that the answering machine is much more efficient than smoke signals."

Sandra liked Martin White Horse a lot. In some ways, he reminded her of her parents, who appeared to be flighty as butterflies but managed to exist and flourish.

"I have one more question," she said. "There's no legendary basis for your part in all this, Martin. I don't recall any mention of a wise Navajo man who engineered my return to the ranch. Why did you do it?"

"Sometimes destiny needs a little shove." He winked at McCloud. "The rest is up to you."

As Martin returned to his men, he was grinning with the pleasure of a battle easily won. Sandra and Mc-Cloud stayed apart from them, watching as the Navajos rounded up the renegades' horses and gathered their equipment. There were a great many remarks and laughter at some of Sandra's purchases.

She leaned against McCloud, fitting her body along the hard contours of his chest and torso. "You know, McCloud, I believe you made an offer to me. Right before you jumped off the edge of the cliff."

"Did I?" he teased.

"You did. And, as your attorney, I'd like to remind you that verbal contracts are legally binding."

Gently he turned her to face him. His turquoise eyes burned brightly. "Sandra, my love, will you stay with me at the ranch? Never leave me again."

"Oh, yes."

With a heartfelt sigh, he embraced her. "It feels like I've waited for an eternity for that consent. And we'll make it work between us, Sandra. Even if you give up your career."

"What?" She bristled. "I have absolutely no intention of giving up my career. I'm not going to abandon everything I've worked for. Not a chance, McCloud. I'll make time to have a law practice and to raise your seven sons."

"My *what?*"

"There's a need for a good lawyer in this part of the country." She glanced over her shoulder at the renegade leader, remembering how they had been terrorized. "Their luck is about to change for the worse."

"Looking for revenge, Sandra?"

"Justice," she said. "I've got my ideals straight. I'll hang out my shingle and start a practice here."

"Your parents will be proud."

"They've always been proud of me," she said softly. "They've always loved me. But I guess this is the first time I've allowed myself to be proud of them."

"You're not so different from your parents, are you?"

"Not in the ways that count." She snuggled against him. "Parents and children sometimes take a long time to really know each other."

"Then I guess we'll have our work cut out for us," he murmured. "With our sons. How many did you say?"

"Seven. That's how many Dawn Fire and her brave had."

"A noble goal," he said. Lightly he kissed her earlobe. "And one that'll be a hell of a lot of fun to pursue."

Sandra agreed. Though she wouldn't attempt to predict the future, she knew she was doing the right thing by staying with McCloud. In their search for a golden city, she had found her own destiny, an unquestioned and joyful fate.

She would stay with McCloud forever. And she would love him for all eternity, until the rivers ceased to flow and the wind through the high grasses was forever silent.

Once in a while, there's a story so special, a story so
unusual, that your pulse races, your blood rushes.
We call this

NANNY ANGEL is one such book.

After one week as a single father, sexy Sam Oliver knows he needs help from the
Guardian Angel Nanny Service to care for his five-year-old daughter. But he isn't
prepared for the blond, blue-eyed out-of-this-world nanny who's about to land on
his doorstep!

NANNY ANGEL
by
Karen Toller Whittenburg

Available in February, wherever Harlequin books are sold.
Watch for more Heartbeat stories, coming your way soon!

MEN MADE IN AMERICA

Fifty red-blooded, white-hot, true-blue hunks
from every State in the Union!

Look for MEN MADE IN AMERICA! Written by some
of our most popular authors, these stories feature some
of the strongest, sexiest men, each from a different state
in the union!

Two titles available every month at your favorite
retail outlet.

In January, look for:

WITHIN REACH by Marilyn Pappano (New Mexico)
IN GOOD FAITH by Judith McWilliams (New York)

In February, look for:

THE SECURITY MAN by Dixie Browning
(North Carolina)
A CLASS ACT by Kathleen Eagle
(North Dakota)

You won't be able to resist MEN MADE IN AMERICA!

HARLEQUIN®

A M E R I C A N ◆ R O M A N C E®

He's at home in denim; she's bathed in diamonds....
Her tastes run to peanut butter; his to pâté....
They're bound to be together....

for Richer, for Poorer

We're delighted to bring you more of the kinds of stories you love,
in FOR RICHER, FOR POORER—a miniseries in which lovers
are drawn together by passion...but separated by price!

Next month, look for

#571 STROKE OF MIDNIGHT
by Kathy Clark

Don't miss any of the FOR RICHER, FOR POORER
books, coming to you in the months ahead—
only from American Romance!

RICHER-1

HARLEQUIN®

AMERICAN ◆ ROMANCE®

Four sexy hunks who vowed they'd never take "the vow" of marriage...

What happens to this Bachelor Club when, one by one, they find the right bachelorette?

Meet four of the most perfect men:

Steve: **THE MARRYING TYPE**
Judith Arnold
(October)

Tripp: **ONCE UPON A HONEYMOON**
Julie Kistler
(November)

Ukiah: **HE'S A REBEL**
Linda Randall Wisdom
(December)

Deke: **THE WORLD'S LAST BACHELOR**
Pamela Browning
(January)

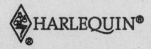

HARLEQUIN®

Deceit, betrayal, murder

Join Harlequin's intrepid heroines, India Leigh
and Mary Hadfield, as they ferret out the truth
behind the mysterious goings-on in their
neighborhood. These two women are no milk-
and-water misses. In fact, they thrive on

MISCHIEF & MAYHEM

Watch for their incredible adventures in this
special two-book collection. Available in March,
wherever Harlequin books are sold.

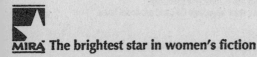

HARLEQUIN®

Don't miss these Harlequin favorites by some of our most distinguished authors!
And now, you can receive a discount by ordering two or more titles!

HT#25577	WILD LIKE THE WIND by Janice Kaiser	$2.99	☐
HT#25589	THE RETURN OF CAINE O'HALLORAN by JoAnn Ross	$2.99	☐
HP#11626	THE SEDUCTION STAKES by Lindsay Armstrong	$2.99	☐
HP#11647	GIVE A MAN A BAD NAME by Roberta Leigh	$2.99	☐
HR#03293	THE MAN WHO CAME FOR CHRISTMAS by Bethany Campbell	$2.89	☐
HR#03308	RELATIVE VALUES by Jessica Steele	$2.89	☐
SR#70589	CANDY KISSES by Muriel Jensen	$3.50	☐
SR#70598	WEDDING INVITATION by Marisa Carroll	$3.50 U.S. $3.99 CAN.	☐ ☐
HI#22230	CACHE POOR by Margaret St. George	$2.99	☐
HAR#16515	NO ROOM AT THE INN by Linda Randall Wisdom	$3.50	☐
HAR#16520	THE ADVENTURESS by M.J. Rodgers	$3.50	☐
HS#28795	PIECES OF SKY by Marianne Willman	$3.99	☐
HS#28824	A WARRIOR'S WAY by Margaret Moore	$3.99 U.S. $4.50 CAN.	☐ ☐

(limited quantities available on certain titles)

	AMOUNT	$
DEDUCT:	**10% DISCOUNT FOR 2+ BOOKS**	$
ADD:	**POSTAGE & HANDLING**	$
	($1.00 for one book, 50¢ for each additional)	
	APPLICABLE TAXES*	$_____
	TOTAL PAYABLE	$_____
	(check or money order—please do not send cash)	

To order, complete this form and send it, along with a check or money order for the total above, payable to Harlequin Books, to: **In the U.S.:** 3010 Walden Avenue, P.O. Box 9047, Buffalo, NY 14269-9047; **In Canada:** P.O. Box 613, Fort Erie, Ontario, L2A 5X3.

Name: _____

Address: _____ City: _____

State/Prov.: _____ Zip/Postal Code: _____

*New York residents remit applicable sales taxes.
Canadian residents remit applicable GST and provincial taxes.

HBACK-JM2